# BOYS & GIRLS

### Edited by Paul Burston

GLASSHOUSE
BOOKS

ISBN 9781907536090

# CONTENTS

# FOLDING KITS

# FOLDING KITS

## DAVID LLEWELLYN

They were out there now, on the field, even as the snow came in. The rugby club was a good mile from the laundrette, but he could see them; the players little more than specks of colour moving around on the muddy turf, boxed in on all sides by a meagre crowd of parents and friends.

The snow itself came rolling down the valley like a thunderhead of smoke, as if the grey sky had been dragged into the cleft between the mountains. It swallowed up the details in its wake; first the chimney stack in the old brickworks, then the pump house at the roadside, and finally the field. When the blizzard reached the town the snowflakes looked like flecks of falling ash against the sky.

'Shut that fucking door, will you?' Said his Dad, ''S'fucking freezing.' And Darren got up from the bench and did as he was told.

He hadn't minded the cold breeze coming in. Even in the winter months it was a relief to taste cold fresh air, or to hear the sounds from outside; the cars and the people, kids playing in the street, a hopelessly out-of-season ice cream van trundling along to the tune of 'O Sole Mio'. With the door shut the only sounds were the machines and the radio. The washers with their low and mournful drone, and rising in pitch with every spin cycle to become a howl. The driers never changing in pitch or tempo, just the hum and the thud-thud-thud of clothes tumbling inside the drums. The radio playing the same chart hits, on an hourly rotation.

It was February now, but it had been this way for seven months. Darren had left school with a clutch of failed or barely passed exams, and while most of his friends made the three mile journey to the job centre and the dole queue, Darren joined his Dad in the laundrette. There had been little question of him working elsewhere. One night, when he was in his bedroom, playing Sonic on the Megadrive, he'd listened to his Mum and Dad talking about it. He paused the game and sat perfectly still, and listened to their raised voices.

'He's got no skills,' his Dad had said. 'He's no good with his hands, and he's not exactly brains of Britain, now, is he?'

And Darren wanted to believe that they thought he couldn't hear them.

The arrangement wasn't ideal, not even to his Dad. Though the laundrette was always busy – many of the people on the estate couldn't afford washing machines or driers, or lived in flats too small to accommodate either – it was a small business and would never make a fortune. His Dad had not given him the job in the ambitious hope that the business would one day pass on, father to son, the beginnings of a dynasty. He had given him the job to avoid the shame of his son signing on like all the other kids from the estate. Signing on, claiming benefits, was the greatest shame his Dad could think of, having spent a whole year jobless when the factories had shut and the money had left the valley, like so much rainwater in so many streams and rivers.

The town itself was like a fortress, something built to defend against marauding invaders. Row after row of identikit, flat-roofed houses rising up on the mountainside, and maybe there was a time when their minimalist, functional design seemed modern and adventurous, the lifestyle of the future, but that time had long since passed. Now, when Darren looked at the town from the valley below he wondered if it was meant to keep outsiders out, or the inhabitants in.

The driers were stopping now, all six of them, one by one in sequence. Inside, the rugby kits fell lazily into coloured piles in the bottom of each drum. Darren's Dad looked up from his copy of *The Sun*.

'You can start folding them, now,' he said.

Darren nodded, and he picked up a plastic laundry basket from behind the wooden counter where his father sat. As he set about throwing the kits into the basket, the door opened, letting in an icy breeze. Wilf, one of their regular customers, closed the door behind him and folded his umbrella, stamping his feet three times to shake the slush from his boots.

'Alright, Wilf?' said Darren's Dad.

'Not bad, Steve. Not bad. Alright, Darren?'

Darren looked over at Wilf and nodded his reply without saying a word.

'Taking over the business from your old man, is it?' said Wilf, with a dry and chesty laugh. He said it every time he came in, without fail, his voice made hoarse by a lifetime of smoking, and he always laughed, as if deep down he knew the idea was ridiculous.

The old man crossed the laundrette and dropped a plastic bin-bag full of clothes onto the counter.

'I see the boys are playing down the club,' he said. 'And in this weather. It's starting to stick, and all. Shops'll have sold out of bread and milk if it carries on like this.'

Wilf and Darren's father looked out through the windows. Sure enough, the snow was falling heavily now, the rooftops of the cars outside coated in a thin, crisp layer of white. They could no longer see the valley or the rugby club.

'Still,' said Wilf, 'we had worse when I was playing. Nineteen forty seven… Now that was a bad winter, but we still played Treherbert. And we won. What about you, Darren? You ever thought of playing?'

Darren's Dad didn't give him chance to answer. 'You're bloody kidding, Wilf,' he said. 'He can't throw, catch or run. They wouldn't let him on the bloody netball team.'

Darren smiled weakly. He could have sulked, and sometimes he did, but never in front of the customers. They could think what they liked about him, about his ability, or inability, to throw, run and catch, but he wouldn't give his Dad the satisfaction. Instead, he set about folding the kits.

This was the one part of the job that gave him pleasure. Folding the kits. Every week, Sandra Lewis, whose husband Dave managed and coached the team, came in with three big bags full of muddy kits. The practise kits, they called them; old yellow jerseys with frayed collars and cuffs, and white shorts smudged with grass stains that just wouldn't come out, even in a boil wash. She dropped them off on the Friday, and they'd be cleaned, dried and folded by Saturday afternoon, ready for next week's training.

Darren always did the folding because his Dad, despite being the owner of a laundrette, had never learned the art of it. Even so, despite the care and attention Darren paid to the task, there were never compliments. It was just his job; the thing he did; but still he took pride in it. The trick was in folding the sleeves, flattening each one out, getting the angles just right, so that you were left with an almost perfect square topped off by the collar. Then they could be stacked, one on top of the other, until they made a cube of sorts, each one five jerseys thick.

The kits were all the same, of course. At first glance they were indistinguishable; twenty yellow jerseys and twenty white pairs of shorts. Twenty pairs of yellow and black socks. Only somebody who had handled each one with such care could tell the difference, could identify a certain kit without even seeing the number on its back.

Darren knew the number 9 kit by the missing button in its collar and the loose stitching in its side. When he saw the loose threads where the button should be, and the vague opening, not yet big enough to be called a hole, he knew it was number 9 without having to turn it over.

This was the kit worn by Lloyd Lewis, the team's scrum half. Lloyd Lewis, son of Sandra, who dropped off the bags full of kit, and Dave, the coach. Lloyd Lewis, apprentice builder, and the reason his father's vans had been repainted with the logo 'Dave Lewis & Son' last summer.

That summer had been different to the many that went before. It was the summer when they left school and got jobs; both of them with their fathers. There was no time for idling, for wasting away whole days and weeks. They were grownups now, young adults, expected to pay their way, to earn their crust.

The summers before had seen them walking out beyond the town, past the pump house and the brickworks and the chimney. They would walk the snaking road that wound its way around the mountain like a coil, and trace their way along the pebbled path, where once there had been train tracks. There, further along the line, was the shell of a building with just the empty frames of a door and two windows. A small brick shed that had served a purpose once, but which was now derelict; its floor littered with crushed cans and bits of broken bottle, the fragments of weathered glass like gemstones. The vague scent of old smoke and stale piss. The inside walls a kaleidoscope of graffiti; names, dates, and declarations scrawled in marker pen and spray paint.

In this place they felt cut off from the world. The open, empty windows and doorframes might look out onto the valley and the town, but it was as if the world could not see in. This was their place, a whole universe within four brick walls. A place that sheltered them from summer storms and prying eyes.

The things that happened inside the small brick shed were never spoken of outside; neither on the journey there, nor during the walk back. Even when they were there, hidden from view, they barely spoke, and when they did it was in euphemisms.

'So ... do you want to do stuff?'

That was always the question, asked by either Darren or Lloyd. If any more was said, it was a game of language, a subterfuge of words. They talked of girls from their school in lustful details, and though those girls might not have been there, they imagined out loud that they were, as if their imaginary presence gave license to each act.

The summer before had been the end of that. At first, Darren thought they might meet up on weekends, on Sundays, perhaps, and walk along the line again, but they didn't. Lloyd had learned to drive and bought himself a car. He'd discovered pubs, and older friends who drank in them. He had neither the time nor the need to walk along the line with Darren. They had barely spoken to one another in the seven months since they finished school.

Of course, Darren could have gone to the pubs, done his best to ingratiate himself with Lloyd's new friends, but he didn't. He had no wish to. His eyes were on the city. At night he would look out from his bedroom window, and though they were black against the night sky, the mountains stood out as silhouettes, the canopy above them an infernal shade of orange lit up by the city lights beyond.

He would save his money, he decided. A little every week. No new games for the Megadrive. No new music. No new clothes. He would save his money and then, when summer came, he would go out in the city. He would go by himself, if needs be. Catch the bus and then the train and go out in the city that lay on the other side of the dark mountains.

And he thought about that now as he took the number 9 jersey, tucking in the sleeves just so, folding it into a near-perfect square. His finger brushed the loose stitching in its side and the hanging thread where a button should be, and then he placed it with the others in a neat and perfect pile.

'Anyway, Steve, I'd best be off,' said Wilf. 'I'll be round Monday to pick 'em up.'

'Tara, Wilf,' said Darren's Dad.

Wilf shuffled off across the laundrette, pausing to look out at the snow 'Still bloody snowing,' he said. 'Can't even see the rugby club no more.'

Then he pulled open the door, and stepped out into the street, and Darren watched him walk away before returning his attention to the kits.

'You wanna get a bloody move on with that, too,' said his Dad. 'Sandra'll be round any minute. It's not like you're working in fuckin' Harrods, now, is it? They'll all get chucked in the back of the car anyway.'

But Darren carried on as he had done before, folding each remaining kit with the same care and attention, taking pride in the precision of his work. Each kit, he imagined, was another penny earned, and another penny saved, and soon enough the snows would melt, the skies would clear, and it would be summer again.

# THE
# UNBEARABLE
# BEAR

# THE UNBEARABLE BEAR

## PAUL BURSTON

The bear isn't a morning person. 'Please don't speak to me in the morning,' he growls, then proceeds to make half a dozen calls on his mobile phone while I sit quietly sipping my coffee. I find myself wondering how six telephone conversations can be less taxing than one face to face communication, but I don't say anything. It's his place, his rules, and I'm crap at confrontation. If I was any kind of animal, I'd probably be a chicken.

The bear comes alive in the afternoon, when he goes to the local gay beach and has sex with strangers. He hopes today's stranger will be tomorrow's live-in boyfriend, and is confused and angry when things don't work out the way he planned. I remember reading somewhere that grizzly bears spend a few days getting to know one another before mating finally occurs. Perhaps the bear would have greater success at finding a mate if he exercised similar restraint? Then again, I also read that the bond between grizzly bears usually lasts for several days or a couple of weeks at most, so maybe they're not the best role models.

The bear and I have known each for a few years, but it's the first time I've observed him in his natural habitat. The last time he visited me, he complained bitterly about some mutual friends who'd recently stayed with him and drunk all the alcohol in his house. Since the bear doesn't drink, and is constantly urging me to finish off the bottles of vodka left by previous guests, I'm beginning to wonder if our mutual friends were really so badly behaved or were simply following orders.

The bear is fond of giving orders. Several times a day he reminds me to lock the door when I go out, to answer the phone in case he calls while I'm in, or to stack the dishes in the dish washer and take out the garbage. I arrived in Barcelona three days ago as a house guest. Now I'm starting to feel more like a housekeeper.

The bear used to be the kind of person who could afford a housekeeper. He was once a bountiful bear who made lots of money and had lots of friends. Now times are tight and he has less money and fewer friends. His closest friend is a woman who bears a startling resemblance to Donatella Versace. Like the bear, she is currently single.

It was she who came up with the nickname 'The Unbearable Bear'. I think it may have started off as a term of endearment, but now the cracks are starting to show and tempers are frayed. She and the bear squabble like an old married couple. Sometimes when she phones he pretends he isn't home. Then she'll try another number, and another.

The bear has several phones. There's the landline that he rarely answers but expects me to pick up on the off chance that it might be him calling and not some total stranger talking in a language I don't understand. There's the work mobile which he uses to call home or send texts urging me to pick up the phone. And there's the iPhone which he uses for everything from photographing men at the beach to sending messages on Facebook to other men he finds attractive.

Today, one of the bear's Facebook friends is flying in from the Middle East on his way to Sitges. The bear is very excited about this. As soon as he's finished making his phone calls and drinking his coffee, he calls me over to look at pictures of his friend on the computer. The man in the photograph is certainly handsome, but I can't help wondering if his expectations of today's rendezvous are anything like the bear's.

As tactfully as I can, I suggest that Facebook might not be the best place to go looking for a boyfriend. Especially one who lives thousands of miles away.

'Don't be ridiculous,' the bear says. 'We met already. We were together in Mykonos.'

Of course. How silly of me. Last month the bear was in Mykonos, where he made a lot of new friends and posted their photos on Facebook. I hadn't realised that this was one of those new friends.

'So what happened?' I ask cautiously, thinking of all those men on the beach and all the great love affairs that failed to blossom.

'We kissed,' the bear says proudly. He doesn't elaborate any further, so I'm left to work out for myself if this was simply a friendly kiss or one that held the promise of something more passionate.

'Great,' I reply. 'Good for you. Shall I make us some more coffee?'

'I don't have time,' the bear sighs. 'I have some appointments and then I have to go to the supermarket and then to the airport.'

'Why don't I go to the supermarket for you?' I suggest. 'You can write me a list.'

The bear considers this for a moment. 'No,' he says finally. 'It's better if I go. You can stay and tidy up the apartment.'

So the bear goes to take a shower and get dressed and I start clearing up the breakfast things and loading them into the dishwasher. Before he leaves, the bear suggests a list of chores that might help me pass the time until he returns home. These range from taking out the garbage and tidying up the sun deck to cleaning the oven and vacuuming the floor. Which are exactly the sorts of things you want to be doing when you're on holiday and it's thirty degrees outside.

'I want everything to be nice for them,' he stresses.

'Them?' I say. 'I thought it was the man from Mykonos?'

The bear looks at me the way a frustrated teacher might look at a particularly dim-witted child. 'He is travelling with friends,' he sighs. 'Two boys and a girl. So there will be four people. Now I must go.'

I decide to tackle the oven first. I can't find any oven cleaner, so I make do with an old scourer and some washing up liquid. I scrub and scrub, but it soon becomes apparent that this oven hasn't been cleaned in quite a while. By the time I'm ready to give up it's almost noon, so I tell myself that I really shouldn't go out in the mid-day sun and turn my attention to the vacuuming. Afterwards I jump into the shower and cover myself in sun lotion before venturing out onto the sun deck. It's a beautiful day and I make short work of tidying up the bar area and hosing down the deck before collapsing on a sun lounger with a book by Marian Keyes. The book is called *This Charming Man*. The irony isn't lost on me.

I'm a few chapters in when I hear voices downstairs. Moments later the bear appears, followed by three men and a woman. The woman announces that she's feeling ill, though apparently this hasn't affected her capacity to chain smoke. Two of the men are clearly a couple. Everything about them is perfectly matched, from their designer shorts to the disdainful expression on their faces. They look me over, decide I'm not worth talking to, and turn their attention back to the bear. The third man I recognise from the bear's photos. He smiles and says hello. Grateful for a friendly face, I say hello back.

The bear is at the bar fixing drinks and I can tell from the way his eyebrow are knitted together that he isn't entirely happy. I go over to help.

'You forgot to take out the garbage,' he mutters.

'Right,' I say. 'Sorry.' He still doesn't look too happy so I add, 'I can take it down now if you like?'

'No,' says the bear. 'I have to go out. I will take it.'

'Where are you going?' I ask.

'To buy a lemon,' he replies, as if the purchase of a single lemon from a shop a short drive away were the most natural thing in the world. 'You must stay and entertain our guests.'

Evidently, our guests are none too keen on this idea. The woman stubs out her third Marlboro and announces that she's going to lie down. The couple decide that they want to go shopping. The bear offers to drop them off on his way to buy a lemon.

Soon they're gone and I'm left alone with the third man, the one the bear kissed on the beach in Mykonos. He tells me his name is Yusef and we chat about his recent holiday and his life in Dubai. He tells me he works for an investment bank and earns a good salary, which makes up for the fact that, in Dubai, homosexuality is illegal. I'm not sure who he's trying to convince – himself or me – but he seems pleasant enough and we pass the time chatting about this and that.

Then the bear is back. Judging by the look on his face, the acquisition of a lemon hasn't helped to lighten his mood. He stands at the door with the lemon in one hand and a glass of ice in the other. I'm not sure what he intends to do with the lemon, but something tells me that he's none too familiar with the concept of taking lemons and turning them into lemonade. I suggest to Yusef that maybe he should go and spend some quality time with our host, and they both disappear downstairs.

I settle back into my book. The tensions of the day are starting to take their toll and I'm happy to follow the publisher's advice and 'Trust Marian'. I'm a long way from home, with a bear with a very sore head, and things are becoming more Kafkaesque by the hour. Compared to this, a tale of domestic violence in Ireland seems strangely comforting.

Yusef and the bear are gone for a good forty minutes, which suggests to me that they must be getting intimate. I hope so anyway. The bear seems to think that sex with Yusef is a done deal, and I don't think he would handle the rejection well.

Suddenly Yusef appears. He has the flushed and cocky appearance of a man who has just had sex. Perhaps now the bear will be a little more bearable.

'Okay?' I ask.

'Okay,' Yusef grins, confirming my suspicions.

I look for the bear. 'Where's...?'

'Downstairs,' says Yusef, and spreads himself out on the sun lounger next to mine. He's less hairy than the bear, and more muscular. I can't decide if he's a bear cub, a muscle bear or possibly even an otter. In the bear world, these distinctions are a potential minefield. In *this* bear's world, *everything* is a potential minefield.

'What are you reading?' he asks.

'Marian Keyes,' I reply.

He looks at me blankly.

'She's really good,' I say.

He doesn't look convinced, so I smile politely and go back to reading my book. Finally I can relax, confident in the knowledge that Yusef has delivered the goods and spared us both any further torment.

Only I'm wrong. Suddenly the bear appears and tells Yusef his taxi is on the way.

Yusef looks confused. 'But my friends – they're still shopping'.

'You must go now,' the bear growls. He goes to wake the sleeping woman, who appears moments later in a cloud of cigarette smoke. She coughs and mumbles something to Yusef, who rolls his eyes and mumbles something back. Then they're both ushered out.

When the bear returns, I ask him what happened.

'Like you don't know,' he snaps.

'I *don't* know,' I reply as calmly as I can. 'That's why I'm asking.'

'He was all over you,' the bear says.

'What?'

'He was all over you, just now.'

'He was just being friendly,' I say.

The bear snorts. 'What are you, stupid?'

'No,' I say. 'And I'm not the one who just had sex with him. I take it you did have sex?'

'Yes we had sex', the bear growls. 'But then he came and talked to you. He should have stayed with me. Why would he have sex with me and not stay with me?'

I resist the urge to say something I might regret. 'You'll have to ask him,' I say.

The bear looks at me like I'm some evil interloper, hell bent on ruining his last chance of love. He looks so wounded, so convinced of his own innocence, I have to remind myself that I haven't actually done anything wrong.

'I must go now,' he sighs. 'I will call you in a few hours. You must pick up the phone. Then you can call a taxi and come and meet me.'

'Okay,' I say.

As soon as the bear is gone, I go to the computer, log onto the internet and book myself into a hotel. Then I pack my bags and leave. No confrontation. No explanation. No note. Yes, I really am a chicken.

# BLOOM

# BLOOM

## JOE STOREY-SCOTT

this is me eighteen nineteen maybe

it's a beautiful day I met this boy there's this boy the most beautiful eyes -sneaked looks quick glances- contact registers we're on the same level and I'm wanting to get it on *how old are you what do you like doing is it safe here* no it wasn't like that something else something could be real jumpstart sidle up and start talking HELLO a rose tattoo upon his neck baseball cap with slouchy look the most beautiful did I mention his eyes he's a hunger all inviting YOU LOOK DELICIOUS is what he says and I'm laughing: he's so hot and I'm just yearning / want to make this and take this much further but this won't happen there are problems, he's got to be someplace somewhere back in the real world in his real life – running, not running with this / all these STUPID PROBLEMS the idea of being, another, he's got / I want to take these things and make them much closer I want but he won't: this is how I suppose it started and sort of ended

and it's later two weeks on it's HOME ALONE now early evening I get ready Status Update: is thinking about going out (and says that and is definitely going out) –getting ready I'm thinking about what I'm wearing and will I see him I might see him again *he could be out tonight* this needs a soundtrack: turn the dial press Music press Artist press Album press Play I

27

wander round in little bits and pieces small hanging all lit up SMELL THE
FLOWERS and look nice What's On Your Mind? I done tons of stuff
but nothing real / need to be smart and so sexy I'm thinking tight centred
and cool with the day-glo / make some choices and I'm ready –phone's
ringing: You Have One New Message *and the promise of something new*

I'm out and it's later meet up and we're crammed tight in the back of a bar
round a table all friends and friends and people I'm not that sure,,,, phone
device out in the palm of someone's hand tapping stroking glow lights up
their face – I don't know who they are don't know if they're with us or
not – lots of catching up to do and the chatting trading light piss-takes
and outrage CHEERS drinks bought all round I look up *and I see him* he's
here in the bar now looking WORLD AROUND ME slows down and
the SHARP FOCUS PULL – Is that that boy asks someone looking over
my shoulder I don't need to look round I know who they mean – Yeah
yeah – a little smile abashed and I'm certain, maybe thinking, did I say
too much and jinx this by talking to others about him too soon –he looks
busy looking round the place not looking over my way so it's obvious he's
decided not to see me at all ALL MY FRIENDS they're probably thinking
I don't know what I'm doing *I don't know what I'm doing* I guess nothing
much happened between us but we met! and he smiled and he knows who
I am maybe there's something could be something ongoing going on Press
Esc To Exit Full Screen Mode *my budding romance* whatever else –drinks
are pushed around the table people talking I'm aware of and I'm back with
them now –said, I put some stuff up on youtube you should see it it's cool
–saying, When I got back there they'd already gone I couldn't find them
–saying, I can't believe that she'd see him after all they went through – so

the boy mr rose tattoo he's forgotten about for now just tucked down the back for la—

someone bumps into me more drinks again hi cheers CHEERS I'm not even sure that I like this place full of dry air and the strong perfumes, someone has their sunglasses on I couldn't do that looks stupid and somehow cool – the music to be seen in and THE MUSIC / on the bar tall vase of white lilies towering the music makes things better but it feels like some scene something everyone's in on not me this seemed like a good idea some other time then the song / song that's playing now I hear it and I'm smiling quick grin then frown it's the song that was playing the time we first met when I met him so I wonder if he's thinking what I'm thinking if he remembers this too he's just over there in the middle WTF – Status Update: it's still So Far, No Sign – it would be easy SO EASY he could just glance over and see me recognise me and smile continue the song where we left things unended here more drinks again cheers cheers and chink glasses - said I got their new album it's so great have you heard it –said I thought it wasn't out yet –said it isn't –DID HE SAY THAT someone stands and group together for a photo opportunity face SMILING everyone all hand gestures and grinning then back to each other the conversations KEEP TALKING I look away and see two people maybe couple all eager to be seen making their way up to the bar they smile and wave over - I'm elated - means nothing, all these people I'm below of and want to be with all they love is to laugh at the bad luck of others I'M ITCHING more friends join us for a minute or two making vague plans to maybe hook up later in this club we might go to then there's more drinks You And 2 Others Like This and some more drinks and I'm drinking the floral shirt that he's wearing it looks new / someone saying are we staying here –said where's my bag oh okay –saying what about that new place IT'S ON but I want to stay here he's still here still blanking me he won't be in that new place I'm sure it's rubbish anyway or maybe he will be –said you're dealing with your life now pal gotta make a decision –said whatever –said what –said you just need to save in this format –said make it better / Then there's movement and people shuffling round the table to be out of here to get ready for the next part of our night ah who decided and when

nnnnnn I'm saying maybe just one more quick one here but everyone's standing I'm still sitting so I guess they win out it's on the way –saying let's go –said don't want to get there too late –said it'll be heaving / and finish up drinks me feeling slightly annoyed a little panic creeping in the music has changed now he's still here still the same –I'm just going to –I need a quick pee first, – meaning I get to walk by his table and give him the chance to see that I'm in here we can catch up maybe it's just that he hasn't noticed me yet yes that's it A Program Needs Your Permission To Continue so I'm weaving my way through the bar it's much busier now guessing which way others will move so to avoid any collision I'm a little drunk now I hesitate as I approach their table he's with his friends they're talking loudly and laughing one has petals from a flower twirl round in their hand I move to the side to let someone get by me I just stand there out in full view it's stupid and awkward and makes me self-conscious but I have his attention he sees me now none of the others notice all wrapped in their thing no-one knows what I am anyway busy laughing with each other having a good time not him FOR A SECOND he lets his eyes lock on mine then as quickly away meaning no don't go there not here oh

I move quickly my way past all these idiots too many people – pushing
my way to the toilets nod hello to some guy coming out I should stop for
a moment and say HI but there's other people going in and out all the
time and we'd be in the way I'm still bruised from the brush off it's much
brighter in here STOP some time-out I step up and piss long and hard
I hadn't felt the need someone's scrawled something on the wall in front
about a club promoter I know -- it's probably true – the bloke along from
me talking into his phone as he pisses clearly proud of the large cock he
makes no attempt to shield / I still expect hope for him to rise from his
table his friends and follow me in here all urgent to explain and validate
what's between us all that we feel Windows Has Identified A Problem
And Unexpectedly Quit –none of his friends know about him WHAT'S
GOING ON it'll be alright we could be together there's still time for
anything tonight –instead this guy I once slept with few months ago
comes in and I try to remember can't recall how things were when we left
it AWKWARD I sort of smile nod to cover the bases and hurry out like I'm
needed to be somewhere fast – thin smiles stretched out when I get back
to my friends not a mean way I attempt some illusion I'm in control taking
TALKING right are we ready are we going let's go

Sometimes there are other times in the dark, outside. Some places taken
over and thrum with a new purpose. Out of the stillness there is movement
and figures make themselves known. Men gather to improvise, inspire and
elicit empty bursts. Everyone watches, everyone waits, every one of us
judging and graded ourselves. How old are you, what are you into, is it

safe here? Eyes flicker in silent transactions, no-one speaks. Each of us out on offer, only want what we need. I control and contain this. Connections, and nothing.

then we're in here it's later in this club and I feel like I'm out on display no one's looking syntax error PLAY THE NEW REMIX the ink-stamp on my hand a daisy shows I'm down in here out clubbing and will prove this in the morning so more drinking say hi, SMILE HI more drinking more drinking this place looks like a fake world and I want to be out somewhere real still THE MUSIC music louder booms hold tight smothers everything some blanket sound –it feels like it's coming from within me there's laughing and talking people drift in and out of / my friends are off mixing –the air in here much warmer and thicker I'm drunk could be drunker I've no idea how I got here and lean on the bar looking for more try to look cool without looking like I'm trying someone stands near me I know them from somewhere and should talk but without knowing why I choose to ignore him / him turning the other way sips his drink makes it clear that it's him ignoring me I don't really care his trousers are hunched low I can see his underwear

I drift off to the dancefloor pretending to look for the friends I lost earlier soon as we got here they've gone off on their own adventures in search of something else something more the music and lights thump really loud Become A Fan Of This things stutter they slow down as smoke fills the room giving me something a minute to hide in I try to dance and make vague moves more or less fit in with the music this music and sound smoke clearing *then I spot him* he's standing on the edge by the tall speakers with his friends from before I can see the bass punch the air *how long* has he been here I need something to think of I can't handle this now I want a cigarette need something to hold onto I head back to the bar not seeing the people and stuff around me I don't want another drink more drinks no maybe I do the music's really loud did he see me maybe that was nothing am I stupid or what mmmh yes yes I would cos it's him that I want the moment we met eyes delicious really beautiful I know there's something just need to get things in place this club is so big and sprawls underground I think I need to get out of here now everywhere just looking I turn the corner and he's standing right there all things stop

for a second so how does this go he's nervous it's happening he looks all around he says they're all leaving he says his friends have all gone he says he told them he was staying on here he could stay here hang with me it's all okay now the music so loud we get drinks we sit down a too-low table with too-low chairs in a corner our drinks clink on the glass top this club / the bar earlier / who we know / where we're going / mutual friends and the music I've no idea what we talk about all I hear are the sounds we sit in every position every limb sending signals scared that some touch will give a wrong meaning THE MUSIC so loud every moment hesitates everything else is forgotten loud music just him with me in here it's cold maybe that's why I'm shaking he frowns looking straight at me looking this matters to him too FALL MADLY *sometimes the lines waver and that's where the beauty is* I can't do this he's saying he can't do this breaks away smiling make a joke out of it out of himself this just to let him get away with it all not connecting not making this real I feel like I want to want to run away but I don't we're still talking he's closer much closer again I stare at his tshirt with the nipple pushing hard we're talking saying nothing his face close to mine I'm drunk and it's late the music is louder a million miles away now it's so quiet and his breath lips smile moving closer we move closer make things clear shift closer his eyes meeting mine move closer so loud eyes move to my mouth smile hesitant the music lips touching like flowers burst out everywhere all around in here the first kiss

tonight

# LISTENING OUT FOR THE SEA

# LISTENING OUT FOR THE SEA

## KEITH JARRETT

'You're a beautiful young man.'

Samuel watches Dr Glenn's feet, the older man's chair scraping on the wooden floor towards him as he speaks. Dr Glenn is now so close he can rest the fat worm of his pointing finger on Samuel's knee. The room feels smaller every second.

Samuel meets Dr Glenn's gaze and then drops his eyes back down, until they are fixed on the finger, which then becomes a whole hand, firmly grasping his leg. He squeezes Samuel's leg briefly then leaves the hand there for a moment that feels uncomfortably long. Samuel can feel Dr Glenn's eyes on him and his squashed mouth ready to continue speaking; for now, though, all he can hear are the seconds on the clock as they sit in silence. Samuel has no idea what he's meant to say.

If his mother wasn't behind the door, he would have considered taking Dr Glenn's hand higher, higher up the lap ladder until he could close it around where he's already beginning to uncurl for action, and only then would he shout loudly, *how dare the perving faggot touch him*, and run out. He would run and not stop; ever.

That's not exactly how it was that time with Anthony Seager; not exactly, but almost. Even after all the days they spent out together on their bikes, up and down Manor Gate looking out for an easy *lift*, with their caps to one side, he couldn't change what happened. Everyone at Buckleys' knew the code: cap one side is danger, the other side ok; and the two of them were dangerous, always. They'd made legends of themselves that spread around school in whispered wows. Anthony with the scissors, jumping off his bike to snip off a shoulder bag, while he was already peddling ahead waiting for the throw. How they bumped several Year 8s, selling them cut up leaves for twenty at time, while they toked, sniffed and swallowed cocktails of gear so mind-fuckingly strong that a) they must have a direct link-up in Amsterdam and b) they were lucky to be alive.

It was the purple buds that did it. The unusually hot afternoon when they bunked school and lay down on the Marshes, puffing Os that disappeared up into the clouds through the long grass, golden brown. They were half-hidden there, voices drowned out by the traffic behind them and yapping dogs ahead, where the flat ground was. Anthony's sweat-soaked school shirt was draped over his bike but Samuel kept his on, dark grey patches trickling down the sides.

'You know what?' Anthony had said, rolling his head towards him and knocking his cap off in the process.

Anthony's hand strayed onto his shoulder, light and playful. Samuel felt his heart do a double-tap. The sun beat down on his head as he relit the weed and took a drag.

They looked at each other for a while, Samuel taking in the zigzag of Anthony's cane row hair and his uneven ears, sticking out like trophy handles. The silver stud on his left earlobe, the shape of a tick, flashed bright in the sunshine. Anthony stared back at him. The dogs in the distance barked louder.

'Yep' Samuel answered after a long pause, exhaling smoke at the same time. He got up to lay on his side so he could pass back the blunt.

'You're such a eediot! "Yep!"' Anthony laughed him off as he waved a fly away, turning his head from him.

Samuel's hand hovered over Anthony's body, waiting for a reaction.

Anthony took the joint from the boy's extended hand after a while. As their fingers brushed, a tingle – just a small jolt of electricity – carried itself up the boy's arm. He put his hand back down on the damp ground and tried not to notice how close it was to Anthony's bare chest, which already seemed darker after just one day in the sun. He tried to avoid thinking about how tight Anthony's stomach looked, wisps of hair disappearing down into his trousers. He tugged at a clump of grass, and a few stalks broke off in his fist.

*Shit*, he thought. I'ed never before allowed Anthony to rise to the front of his mind while they were together. Not in *that* way. *Allowing to rise. So high these thoughts are rising to the sky. Letting my mind drift with the spliff*... Samuel kicked the rest of his thoughts away with a freestyle rhyme, and soon he knew he would be spitting bars with Anthony and they would be joking together, as soon as he could temporarily bring his dry mouth to open, as soon as he had the strength to sit up and roll another. And he could forget the eye contact and the rise and fall of Anthony's belly and daydreams of them fucking.

When Samuel nodded his head back to the ground, he caught Anthony's eyes again. Their bodies seemed closer; Anthony's diamond eyes carving deeper into his head, eyes that were fixed on him.

It was Samuel's hands that did it; not him. His hands which wandered all the way down from Anthony's belly button to his belt loops and to the bulge in his trousers, even though it wasn't safe, right there, in the open where anyone could pass through if they were following the smell of their smoke. But then mouths were pressed over lips, and hands explored beneath waistbands.

It all felt natural and real until Anthony pulled away and said what he said.

'I see it's been hard for you.' Dr Glenn smiles, his saggy cheeks pushing outwards, but lips still pressed together. 'There's a lot of guilt... and shame there,' he says, removing the hand from Samuel's knee and tapping his own heart loudly with a knuckle.

There's a moment in which the boy feels his eyes get hotter, and then he breathes in and it goes. The air in the room is all wrong; the mean windows are wide open but it feels like he's suffocating.

'But there's no need for you to feel guilty about these feelings anymore –'

'How can I – ?' the thin, squeaking voice leaks out from him.

'"There is therefore now no more condemnation to them which are in Christ Jesus, who walk not after the flesh, but after the Spirit."' Dr Glenn pauses and sucks in all the air that is left in the room. 'Romans 8:1. The last bit is the key', he continues. 'Now you are in Christ Jesus, you no longer have to walk after the *flesh* – you can be free from it.'

Dr Glenn's peanut-shaped head bounces side to side as he speaks, and he slides up his glasses with the same wormy finger that was on his knee minutes ago. *You're a beautiful young man.*

The boy wonders about being free. The moment before Anthony told him, he felt free; lying on the grass in September, the unexpected heat which made going to school that day too stupid an idea. Free for a second, knowing that he would get into big trouble for bunking again; knowing that his mother would drag him to the Pastor again; and not knowing yet what Anthony was about to say, just a few small words he couldn't erase,

*I was hoping you'd do that a long time ago.* Like he'd been waiting for him, setting a trap. All along, Anthony had been the batty boy. Anthony had egged him on to skip school with him, hang out and play video games at his house on the weekend and check girls near Mad Riddims, where they spent their money on mix tapes, for what?

Samuel replayed it in his head: a shout, coming from them both; the sound of his fist on a face he'd just kissed; feeling his shirt being pulled, choking around his neck; looking for something to hold onto; the pain of bite marks; the pulse throbbing in his hand, and then, later, the thud in his head as he remembered the look on *Anthony's face.*

All along, it was Anthony who'd been checking him out. Anthony had picked him out as a friend not because he was smart but because he'd already planned that afternoon. It made him sick. Everyone must have been laughing behind his back.

By the end of that day, he'd already decided to get some more of the Buckley boys in on it before Anthony did; he'd need back up for next time.

'There's nothing wrong with you. Nothing that you yourself have done which caused you to have these feelings ', Dr Glenn says, from a faraway place. 'They're just feelings, not who you are... Don't let anyone tell you otherwise'.

Dr Glenn is leaning forward again and staring him in the eyes. He comes into focus mid-sentence.

'I see you have the power to overcome this—this *affliction* and develop into a great young man. And this power comes from the Holy Spirit'.

Samuel wonders whether all the lifting and smoking he's done has sucked the Holy Spirit from him for good, even though he's prayed every night that God would forgive him. Maybe that's why he hasn't yet changed into who he should really be. *Normal.*

He wonders what his mother can hear through the door, and if he would be able to make out her shape through the frosting if he turned around. He knows she has her ears pressed closely against the door like a shell, like she's listening out for the sea.

Dr Glenn is looking at him again. He has the same thin-lip smile on him, like he's waiting for Samuel to say something. He could talk about Anthony forever, but it's still too heavy in his gut.

Samuel's energy was taken up with hating him, after that day. *It wasn't Samuel's fault.* He just got there first. He had to get the Buckley boys on his side quick time, otherwise it would have been him that got beat down. For a long time afterwards, he spent hours sleeping, trying to make himself feel nothing.

He'll never see Anthony again.

He'd written down how he'd felt in an exercise book, a continuous freestyle riff about the two of them sketched in red ink; now, there's nothing more to say. What he wrote in the book – just scribbles – ended up in his mother's hands when he fell asleep holding it. He half-knew it would happen one day; he was almost glad she knew, even though it meant coming here to see Dr Glenn so that he could be healed.

He knows that when he comes out from the room, she'll study his face, hoping for signs of change. It makes him want to sink lower in the wooden chair, until he disappears into it. He looks up again.

'Would you like to pray with me?' Dr Glenn asks.

Samuel nods.

'Dear Jesus', he begins and Samuel drifts into the familiar pattern of words he has spoken before. For a moment, he feels free again, believing he can change.

# EXIT THROUGH THE WOUND

## NORTH MORGAN

On Monday evening I'm attempting to pack for my trip back home, and if I were writing this the word 'home' would be in quotation marks, because I'm packing to go back to the place where I grew up and where my parents still live, all four of them, the place where I grew up but I haven't lived in for twelve years, the place that I haven't visited for sixteen months, and I suppose maybe this counts as home, but I'm not so sure. Because home is Athens, Greece, a place where I heard a young cousin around my age tell a family gathering that if his son were gay he would 'slaughter him on his lap', a place where I was bullied out of school for being gay at the age of 11, when I didn't even know myself, but several of my schoolmates inexplicably already did.

So I'm in my house in Bayswater, my big empty house, my big empty cold house that Dad bought for me and Brendan comes over and when he walks through the door he finds me standing in front of an almost empty suitcase, but against a brick wall really, indecisive, unable to figure out what I need to put in there. At this point, the only contents of the suitcase are a copy of *The Catcher in the Rye* and a copy of *Less Than Zero*, two books I could think of about being reunited with your family right before Christmas, about going back home (with quotation marks). Brendan takes and a look and tells me this urban legend about *The Catcher in the Rye*, tells me that it's one of these books that's associated with the reader committing suicide, so I take it out of the suitcase and put it in my hand luggage, then ask him what else he thinks I should pack.

I explain that I can't decide between all the clothes, because I can't decide who I want to be when I go back home, who I want people to think that I am. And Brendan tells me that maybe I should just be myself ('Be yourself', he says). So I reply that I'm not sure who that is anymore, and I continue to stare, both at a mostly empty suitcase – contents: one book now – and a closet full of different versions of me, or who I am meant to be.

That's when my Mum calls and asks me how the packing is going and what food I eat these days so she can arrange it for me when I get there – and then tells me that she has some bad news which she hasn't told me yet, but I'll have to know sooner or later. I tell her to hit me, and she says that her sister, my aunt Catherine, has died. So I ask how it happened and when the funeral is and Mum tells me that she couldn't fight it anymore ('She lost the battle', she says) it happened two weeks ago, the funeral has already taken place, it's all over now.

This is just another in the long series of bad news that my parents have avoided telling me to stop me from being upset, but I guess it works both ways: they don't tell me when close relatives die, I don't tell them that I'm gay, they didn't let me watch the news when I was younger, I don't let them see the tattoos that I'm getting now that I'm older.

Thinking about my lack of self-defenses, I ask Mum to get me some more Xanax when I go back because I'm running low. Mum says 'okay' and we hang up.

I call my big brother and ask him to guess who rang me up yesterday. 'We had a nice chat after having not spoken to each other for such a long time', I say. My brother replies, 'I don't know, who?'. I tell him, 'Aunt Catherine'. My brother tells me I'm a loser and hangs up.

Brendan leaves and I finish packing on my own, because it's now a few hours before my flight and this is what I have to do.

On Tuesday morning I get to the airport, where I check in my bag, buy my parents, step-parents and brother ridiculously expensive presents because it's their own money I'm using anyway, and make my way to the gate.

On the plane and I'm surrounded by hundreds of Greeks who look exactly like the people I went to secondary school with. Maybe some of them are the same people I went to secondary school with, I can no longer tell. Homogeneous, Greek, very dark brown hair, dark brown eyes with black circles, disproportionate noses, stubble three minutes after they've shaved, talking shit. In a life where nothing went the way it was supposed to, at least I can be grateful I bypassed my national genetic code.

With 5mg of Valium having worn off just in time for me to be annoyed by the fact that all the Greek passengers burst into applause as soon as the plane touches the ground (I fly a lot, and this is the only nation that still considers a touchdown to be something so novel or extraordinary you have to applaud it, like they didn't expect it, like the pilot doesn't do this for a living), we land in Athens.

Two of my parents meet me at the airport and as step-dad drives us home it takes him less than 8 minutes to comment on my salary and ask me why I'm not making £60,000 by now. My step-dad's only criterion for measuring people's worth is how much money they make, which isn't a bad one, I suppose, though I also like to take looks into consideration.

Back at home, where I lived from the ages of 8 when my mum remarried to 17 when I left for London, I give my mum, step-dad and my brother the presents I spent too much money on and start pushing my plastic surgery idea hoping they might fork out for it. My mum seems open-minded, my step-dad laughs it off so I guess I'll just have to ask my real dad (who has more money, cares less and sees me more infrequently), do it behind my step-dad's back and turn up with a new face and see if he notices. I explain to my brother the changes I want to make to my eyes and nose and he tells me that if I go ahead with this I'll look too preppy ('You'll look way too preppy', he says), which I understand he means as an insult but I take as the final reassurance I need that I must do this.

I take a shower, go to the bedroom which I've been assigned for this holiday (the bedroom I had when I lived here is now occupied by a running machine, a TV on the wall and nothing else), make a quick phone call to Daniel in California and go to bed.

I wake up on what people tell me is Christmas Day and the weather is unseasonably warm in Athens. It's about 23 degrees, so I put on trousers, a polo shirt and a cardigan, which is not just another way to punish myself, just a way to cover my arms, legs, all the tattoos, most of the shame, and my mum drives me to visit my grandparents. I haven't seen them for a couple of years.

Grandma opens the door, looking composed enough for someone who's just lost a daughter two weeks ago I suppose. She gives me a hug, sits me down and has a little talk where she tells me to take care of myself, that health is the most important thing there is, that I should be my number one priority in life, and that I should avoid eating chickens because they pump them full of hormones and I'm more than likely to grow breasts as a result, and then she goes and digs out granddad.

Granddad hasn't left home for four years now and he's the closest thing to the living dead that I've ever seen. And not the living dead in a good way like in the Suede song of the same name thanks to post-modern, 'I'm-so-bored' heroin use, but the living dead in a bad way because of old age.

Granddad tells me that I've grown since he last saw me (impossible), announces to everyone that I look like Brad Pitt and whispers in my ear a story about having nearly moved to Australia when he was younger to follow some girl, his mother sabotaging him and tearing up the letters the girl had sent him, and how he ended up marrying my grandmother instead.

Then Grandma asks me what I'm planning to do over the few next days in Athens. I tell her that I'm planning to do whatever I want without letting anyone get in the way. Grandma kisses me on the forehead and then we go.

My mum takes me over to my dad's house and drives off before he and my step-mum come out. He and my step-mum come out and we get on our way to Christmas lunch with what, I guess, people refer to as extended family.

On the way to what is possibly a second cousin's house, dad talks and I listen. Dad talks about the state of the economy, family affairs in general, my cousin's working hours, making the perfect steak, brand new property versus property with character, other topics that I forget. It's unclear whether I'm required to provide input in this, so I don't. I don't say anything and instead I sit there nodding at the right points, maybe some wrong ones too, thinking: do I need another tattoo, must go to Iceland again soon, do I have Xanax with me – panic – wait, I do, steroids versus growth hormone, 'Womanizer, woman-womanizer, you're a womanizer', Daniel's lips, Daniel's lips, Daniel's eyes, Daniel's lips.

We get to what I still suspect is a second cousin's house, I get ready for the worst and we go in.

A large part of my family from my Dad's side is quite disgustingly working class. There, I said it, they are working class. This cousin is a taxi driver (a taxi driver!). His wife is … oh I don't know, I really don't. And they have two sons, just a bit younger than me and neither of them has been to university.

Every time I go back home to visit, I meet distant family members like these. So I see these people every 2-3 years on average and the interaction is always the same. Somehow, they take personal offense at my choice to live abroad, working on the assumption that I have rejected them and their lifestyles and that I have some superiority complex. The fact that this assumption is very nearly true doesn't really help.

Of course they are also racist, xenophobic and bigoted, not so much in a malicious, deliberately hateful way, but in the way that characterizes the uneducated working classes. These sentiments naturally hit red when I'm around: a traitor, a stuck up cunt that lives in England, an embarrassment of a country compared to the grandeur and superiority of Greece.

For this Christmas lunch, I mostly get sweaty in a cardigan that I'm too scared to take off and listen to shocking conversations:

My cousin asks me whether everyone in England is ugly and a fag and if all the women are sluts and crap in bed.

My cousin's wife shares the information that the whole of Northern Europe were climbing on trees and feeding on bananas around the same time when the glorious nation of Greeks had invented cutlery and cooked their meat. My cousin adds that they still don't cook their meat in Northern Europe, in fact they eat raw elk and therefore they are very primitive.

When the Muppets adaptation of *A Christmas Carol* comes on TV everyone gets enthusiastic and is amazed by this brand new production. I point out that this film is at least 15 years old but nobody believes me.

When somebody (a cousin I don't recognise?) questions the validity of *A Christmas Carol* featuring the Muppets because it shows Kermit and Miss Piggy as a family with children 'even though Miss Piggy never had children' I point out that it's an adaptation of a Charles Dickens story, not a documentary. My cousin's son picks on the name Charles (an unusual name to Greek ears), makes a connection with Prince Charles, who is English and therefore a fag. Everyone cracks up at this brilliant witticism.

Around that point I drift off, start thinking about my new nose, imagine how amazing it would be to have the Australian personal trainer from my gym as a friend, make a resolution to try harder at the gym in the new year, cancel my resolution to try harder at the gym in the new year because it sounds too superficial, picture Daniel sitting at this Christmas table with me as my boyfriend, try to guess what my relatives would think if they knew I were gay but I have such a handsome boyfriend as Daniel (surely my gayness would be forgiven?), try to replay 'Born To Run' by Bruce Springsteen in real time in my head, plan the evening's TV viewing.

After some course or other I slip into the bathroom, lock the door and sit on the closed toilet lid. In my trouser pockets I find: two vials, one and two thirds Valium tabs (approx 8mg in total), two mobile phones (one pre-paid), a leather card wallet (no cash). In my cardigan pockets I find: a folded print-out of a map of central Athens, four Xanax tabs (10mg each). I crush all the pills, snort them using the rolled up map and lean back.

# DYING, AND OTHER SUPERPOWERS

# DYING, AND OTHER SUPERPOWERS

## KRISTIAN JOHNS

JOSHUA.

I'll remember my eighteenth birthday for three reasons. The first being that I turned eighteen.

Well, duh.

The second reason is because it was the day I got diagnosed with HIV. And the third? I made a mug explode.

Yeah, that was a pretty hectic day.

I suppose I should start by telling you about myself. This type of story always starts with that, doesn't it? Ellie (my best mate) says it's to help people 'connect' with the central character, i.e. me. She reads *Harry Potter* and the *Twilight* stuff, so I suppose she knows what she's talking about.

She's making me write everything down so there's a record of it. I think she wants to make me into some sort of tragic hero when I'm gone. Not that I give a shit. I'm going to be dead aren't I? I don't believe in the afterlife. Mind you, I've definitely been re-evaluating what I do and don't believe in lately.

I'm tall-ish — about 5'11' or 180 centimetres if you're using metric measurement. They make us use metric in school, but my mum's always asking 'what's that in feet and inches?' so I know both.

Lookswise, I'm average, slender, verging on the skinny, although I'm told I'll 'fill out' soon — usually by guys with beer bellies. Great. Looking forward to *that*. Dark hair, green eyes. Told good looking. I'll stop before I start sounding like a lonely hearts ad.

I spend my days at college doing an HND in Business Studies, my evenings playing on my Xbox and my nights having wet dreams about my mum's boyfriend Stuart, who's Daniel Craig's double, and always walks around in tight briefs that purposely show off a pretty hefty cock.

I know it's hefty because I've sucked it. He had big balls, too, despite the fact he uses steroids. He called me into the bathroom to 'chat' once while he dried himself off after his shower. He got hard and I ended up sucking him off for a bit. He wanted to fuck me, but we heard my mum's keys in the front door and I had to dive quickly out of bathroom so we wouldn't get caught. I heard them going at it shortly afterward. Sounded like he was giving her a proper seeing to. I was next door, cock in hand, wishing he'd swing by and do the same to me.

Despite everything that's happened — I still definitely would — despite the fact he's 43 and he's boned my mum.

Anyway, I'm getting distracted.

The HIV thing.

I only meant to go for a while without a condom, but I'm not going to lie — it felt fucking awesome. I mean, it was a compliment really, he just kept saying over and over how good I felt, and yeah — the thought of him coming inside me turned me on, so I let him. He came so hard I could actually feel him shooting inside me.

Jesus, if I could just go back to that night and do it all over again, but safe this time, I would, but you don't think about sitting in a badly decorated NHS consultation room getting told 'the news' by some doctor/nurse/counsellor/whatever when you're straddling some fit 28 year old who's going insane at the fact he's got his bare dick inside you.

But that's exactly where I ended up, four months later on my eighteenth birthday. I knew I needed to get tested. You can hardly pick up a gay mag nowadays without getting saturated with ads begging you to have safe sex. And despite my shit judgement that night, I'm not stupid, I knew what I'd done and I knew what the risks were. I suppose getting tested on my eighteenth was symbolic. 'Officially' becoming a man meant I had to face up to it and stop pretending everything was OK.

I suspected I'd got it. I'd had a nasty bout of flu a few weeks previously and I knew that's one of the symptoms. But it was still a shock. This cute Irish guy, Marco (apparently he had Italian blood), pricked my thumb with a needle and told me to come back in an hour. So I did.

That's when he told me I had HIV. And that's when I made the mug explode.

It happened like this: Marco called me in, smiled, but not too brightly, and invited me to sit down. You could tell he'd done the whole telling people thing a thousand times before. His delivery was perfect. It was matter-of-fact without being too cold and clinical.

'Well, Josh, I'm sorry to say your test came back positive,' he paused, letting me absorb it, 'I'll just give you a second …'

I sat there, blunted. The room swayed. I couldn't hear properly and I didn't know which way was up, like I'd been thrown into a swimming pool. All I could think was: *How am I going to tell my mum?*

Acid belched up from my stomach and into my mouth. My ears had gone pop, everything sounded muffled and slow, like the batteries of reality were running out. I felt this rumbling sensation. My head was tight and I couldn't think — I was panicking. Marco leant forward, put his hand on my arm and said, 'Josh, are you OK?'

I knocked his arm away, and as I did, felt a tightening sensation around my hand, like it was inside one of those inflatable pulse monitors they measure your heart rate with. I shook it instinctively, and the air around it blurred — like a heat shimmer. Beyond it, I noticed Marco's mug on the desk and as I did, the heat-shimmer gathered instant velocity and shot towards it.

And it exploded, and I mean really exploded. Not cracked, not shattered, but genuinely whoops-I-stepped-on-a-land-mine detonated. Great shards of cheap, yellow ceramic hammered into the wall behind the desk, and caused all the papers and files on it to develop coffee coloured freckles. The wall was a river of brown blood.

An open mouthed Marco gawked at me, then back at the coffee drizzling down the shrapnelled wall, then at the closed, intact window behind him, as if to check Lee Harvey Oswald hadn't risen from the dead and cracked off another shot for old time's sake.

I grabbed my rucksack and ran. I heard him shout my name behind me, but I was already running out of the main door. I ran for longer than I should have, I think I ran nearly all the way home. I can't remember. My head felt like it was being drilled into from both temples. I crumpled onto my bed and slept for thirty-six hours solid.

I won't bore you with a long description of what happened when I broke the news of my diagnosis to my Mum, but yeah, it was pretty gruesome. There was a stunned silence, followed by a fair amount of crying, a few angry exchanges, a *lot* of talking and then finally, reassurances that she would support me in any way she could.

I had pretty much the same with Ellie, although she was less diplomatic. She slapped me round the face and called me a stupid cunt, then broke down in tears and held onto me for dear life, as though she expected me to evaporate or drop dead on the spot.

Sometimes I'm so glad I'm gay — girls are weird.

Life went almost back to normal. I almost forgot about the incident in the clinic that day. I certainly didn't tell anyone about it. I carried on with college. Mum ordered a shitload of books on AIDS off the internet and would make a point of turning up the volume if anything about it came on the news. I suppose it was her way of telling me it was alright.

Stuart was totally freaked. I could tell. He started wearing clothes in the house for a start, and there were no more naked, post-shower chats and definitely none of the 'other' stuff. He was clearly relieved at his lucky escape, he'd come within an inch (or about nine) of fucking me that day.

After that he just turned into a dick. He'd grab my mum whenever I walked in the room and get off with her in front of me, as if to prove to me how straight he was. Most of the time he regarded me with barely concealed disgust. I understand all that fake-straight-repressed-sexuality self-hatred crap — really I do, but it still pissed me off.

Things came to a head in more ways than one when I came home to find my mum and him having a full-on slanging match in the lounge.

'I don't care if you want to spend more time with me! My mum was saying hotly, 'He's eighteen years old! He's just been told he has HIV! He needs me! I'm not throwing my son out on his ear!'

Stuart was complaining back, 'All I'm saying is that it's time he started fending for himself, Lorraine, he put his hands on her shoulders in a pretty good impression of someone who gives a shit, 'he needs to stop hanging around with that girl and get some proper mates — you know — people like him, people who —'

'Who what, Stuart?' I asked. They hadn't noticed me standing in the doorway.

He fumbled. 'Josh, hey, mate, I didn't see you there.'

'Clearly. So are you going to finish your sentence?' I lounged casually against the doorframe, 'people who what, Stuart? People who have HIV?'

The reply came instantly, 'I wasn't talking about that.'

I snorted 'Ah, so you mean the *other* thing — people who like getting their dick sucked by other guys, perhaps? Is that what you were talking about? Well we should both find some mates like that, shouldn't we? After all, that type of thing is right up your street, isn't it Stuart?'

I couldn't stop. All the resentment, bitterness, regret, fear and anger at everything that had happened swelled up in me like bile, and I couldn't help myself.

'Oh, no wait, of *course* it's not, because we all know which category *you* belong in, don't we, Stuart? Closet queer! That's right, isn't it? Or did I —'

'— You shut your fucking mouth!'

'— get it wrong? Is it that you like a bit of both? Is the idea of having a mother and her son what turns you on?'

'What is he talking about, Stuart?' my mother's voice chimed in.

'Keep out of this, Lorraine!'

'I will not keep out of this! Don't you tell me what to do! What is he talking about?'

I was yelling now, there was a rumbling noise coming from somewhere, like a low-flying jet, building and getting ever nearer, till it began to drown us out.

'Didn't he tell you, mum? Didn't he tell you about the day I sucked his dick while you were at work? Did he not tell you the only reason he didn't fuck me till his legs buckled was that you came home early?! Isn't that right Stuart?'

'You shut the fuck —'

'Stuart! What is he —'

'— up, you fucking queer cunt!'

'— talking about?'

He whirled on her. 'Just shut your fucking mouth for one fucking second, Lorraine! All you ever do is talk, talk, talk! The only time you shut up is when you've got a cock in your mouth!'

'Don't talk to my mother like that!' I shouted above the rumbling-without-a-source, which was getting louder by the second.

He span back round, his face centimetres from mine. 'Or what, gay boy?' he hissed loudly, 'You want to start with me, do you?'

A vein bulged in his forehead. He looked huge. I think he'd been on the steroids again. His voice grew louder.

'You fucking lying prick! I ought to break your fucking neck for what you just said! You lying, AIDS infested—' He raised his arm to hit me and I flinched.

'YOU LAY ONE FINGER ON MY SON AND SO HELP ME GOD, I'LL —'

'—queerbag piece of shit!'

'—KILL YOU!' My mum grabbed Stuart's raised arm and he batted her away. She came in again and he swung his fist at her, connecting with her cheekbone. She fell back. Hard. Blood already oozing from the cut he'd given her. He went to hit her again.

'GET THE FUCK OFF OF HER!'

My voice boomed out like an explosion, stopping him dead in his tracks. The rumbling became an earthquake. Photo frames and knick knacks rattled a melody on the mantelpiece. A picture fell off the wall — nobody looked at it.

I fixed him an icy glare and walked towards him purposefully. The air seemed to whirl around me, my clothes and hair whipping in the current. My eyes grew hot. I kept advancing.

Stuart just stared at me with a shocked expression on his face. He looked around as if hoping to find someone behind him — the real object of my focus — but I carried on glaring, walking, arms outstretched, pulling the churning air from around me wrapping it like cyclones around my forearms. I was seething with some unseen energy — starting in my toes, a sensation like billions of tiny bubbles travelling upwards over the surface of my skin, up my back, spreading out towards my shoulders and down my arms, building towards a crescendo in my hands. Instinctively I threw them out in front of me, fingers splayed.

The air around my forearms shimmered — the same as before — and I saw... something... shoot from my hands, like an invisible jet of water. I actually saw the air part around it as it rocketed and rippled towards him. It hit him square in the chest and suddenly he was nothing more than a rag doll, flying through the air. My head buzzed, crackling with electricity. Everything seemed to slow right down and I was just a helpless observer, watching Stuart as he floated in slow motion towards the big bay window at the end of the room.

Someone — I don't know if it was me — shouted 'NO!' and the world sped up again. The buzzing in my head became a chainsaw. Stuart shot like a bullet towards the window. I screamed, clutching my hands to my temples — all I could think of was stopping him from smashing through it.

And just liked that, he stopped. And I mean right there, in mid air.

I stood, speechless as he hung motionless for about ten seconds, his eyes bulging at me with a mixture of terror and disbelief. We carried on looking at each other. There was no sound anywhere. Then, I felt a sharp twanging sensation in between my eyes, as if some cord in my mind had snapped, and he dropped to the floor. Sound exploded back into the world. I could hear my mum screaming, a car alarm blasting. Stuart clambered unsteadily to his feet croaking 'What the fuck?!' There was a dark patch on the front of his jeans.

I gaped at my hands, turning them over a couple of times, but my vision was blurring and I felt unsteady. I looked around the room, unfocused and disoriented, and in a weak voice said, 'Mum?'

I don't know if she answered, because my world went black.

I woke up on a thin hospital mattress with an oxygen mask on my face. My mum was sat by my bed with a plaster on her cheek, clutching my hand and looking drawn. When she spoke, her voice was small, quiet.

'They've been taking blood every hour because your white cells are really low; your counts are lower every time they take readings. They think that's why you collapsed. You know, because of your… illness.'

'You can say the word, Mum. It's called HIV, and I think we both know it wasn't to do with that.' I felt guilty for snapping but I needed her to take charge and be my mum, not this feeble, squeaky voiced thing impersonating her.

'Where's Stuart?' I asked.

'He's gone, Josh. Please, darling. I'm dealing with enough at the moment. I just want you to get better and get you home. That's all I want to concentrate on.'

'Mum, you saw me, you saw Stuart. Don't act like it didn't—'

'Josh, *please.*' She looked at me beseechingly. Begging me to allow her the luxury of denial, pleading to stay blind to the truth. And I knew the conversation was over.

After a few days, my white blood cells — or CD4 count — levelled out and they discharged me, but I spent the next two weeks in bed with some sort of flu bug. The doctor said it was probably a viral thing I'd caught in hospital while my immune system was spazzing out. Nothing some rest wouldn't cure.

Mum and I didn't speak about the events of that day again, but Ellie came round to see me after college a lot. At first, she didn't believe me when I told her — but I suppose telling your best mate you're telekinetic is a lot further up the things-that-are-hard-to-accept scale than telling her you have HIV.

But I have to say, I was surprised how long it took her to come round to the idea. Ellie loves anything like that: *Heroes, True Blood, Harry Potter,* she can't get enough of it. I had half-expected her to have me dressed in a cape and tights within a week.

I practised a lot. In my bedroom, after college. I'd line up objects of different sizes and weights and concentrate on them, trying to make something happen. Sometimes I managed to make something roll or fall off the desk, and I could float light objects, stuff like that. Nothing in the same league as a whole person, though. Most of the time I just gave myself a nasty headache. I had a headache most days back then. They usually went away after I'd had a nap. Ellie said she was worried about me.

'You look thin,' she said to me one day. We were lounging on my bed, idly chatting and playing with our phones. I always find it weird how phones have taken over our lives. Ellie and I would always be doing something on our phones, even when we were supposed to be spending time with each other. Sometimes we'd be in the same house and yet be texting each other.

'Better than recently,' I replied. I'd had flu yet again — the second time in a month.

'Suppose. You still look thin, though.'

'Ellie, I already have one mum, I don't need another.'

'I'm just saying. I'm worried about you, Josh. I don't think it's such a good idea, you know… what you've been doing.' Her face grew serious. 'I've been doing some thinking. What if…' she paused, 'what if the virus somehow altered your genetic makeup and is the reason you've developed these … powers? Know what I mean?'

'What a pile of crap.'

'It's not, you know. Think about it. When was the first time your powers manifested?'

'Would you stop calling them that? You make me sound like a prick.'

'OK, *abilities* Jesus You queers are so touchy. Anyway, it was the day you got diagnosed at the clinic, yeah? When you had the panic attack?'

'Well, yeah. But I'd caught the virus way before that. I know who gave it to me, remember?'

'You're missing the point. Before that day, you've had dramas, you got angry, yeah?

'Yeah, but I don't see — '

'Nothing weird ever happened though, did it? You've never made so much as a pencil roll across a desk, know what I mean? So the question you need to ask is: what changed?'

I closed my eyes and sighed, 'Does it matter, Ellie? I'm tired I was at it for three hours today.'

'Yes, it *does* matter, Josh. You can't see it, but it's all linked. And anyway, that's beside the point. Whether or not catching the virus was the cause of these abilities, it's becoming clear that the more you mess around with them, the more you deplete your system. You're going to do some serious damage to yourself if you carry on, and you —'

'Oh, here we go.'

' — need to stop trying to develop it. You've told me yourself it gives you a pounding headache. You were laid up for a fortnight after the whole incident with your mum's boyfriend. You've been ill more times than I can remember in the last few months. Your mum told me the hospital is worried about your CD4 count, you have bags under your eyes and you're so bony I'm scared to hug you in case you snap.'

'Oh, shut up, Ellie, you don't know what you're talking about. You fucking freak.'

'*Me* a freak?' Ellie shot back. 'I'm not the one who goes around blowing up cups of coffee just by looking at them, am I? No. That would be you, as a matter of fact.'

'Just shut up, Ellie!'

'Or what?' her voice sizzled with anger. She stood up and faced me square on, jabbing her finger into my chest, 'Are you going to do your funky little mind-ray thing and blow me to pieces too? Is that what you're going to do, Superboy? Hmm? Well, be careful — we don't want you getting all sick again, do we?'

'Ellie, just shut up.'

She crossed over to the window, throwing her arms up in exasperation 'Grow the fuck up, Josh, you can call it what you like: superpower, freak coincidence, act of God, genetic mutation — who knows? You may have been abducted by aliens and injected with some sort of super-juice for all we know. But whatever it is, you need to get off this little I-want-to-play-superhero trip because it's *hurting* you!'

I rounded on her. 'You think I'm doing this for fun!? You think I want to get dressed up in spandex and fly around the world dragging people out of burning buildings? *You* grow the fuck up, Ellie! I need to get control over it because it TERRIFIES me! I can't walk around scared I'm going to send something into orbit —'

'Josh …' Ellie said my name, trying to calm me down, but I didn't want to listen.

' — or blow it to bits! Something like this should be used to do good in the world, not —'

'Josh, you need to calm —'

' — Will you LET ME FINISH!' My eyes felt hot and my brow was buzzing again, 'I'm scared stiff, Ellie! I feel so alone! It keeps happening and I don't know how to control it! And every time I try to I —'

'JOSH!'

'WHAT?'

'Stay very still and don't move a muscle. Just look.'

I looked around my room.

Every object in it had lifted from where it had stood and was floating half a metre in the air, which had grown humid and heavy with static. I realised I could hear the thrumming, rumbling noise again.

'Don't speak.' she walked slowly back across the room so that she ended up right behind me, speaking gently and hypnotically, like you would to a child, 'Don't look at me. Just concentrate. Concentrate on the things in the room. Hold them there.'

My forehead buzzed harder, like someone was holding an electric toothbrush in between my eyes, but this time it felt different. Rather than the painful, all consuming sensation I'd had before, where the normal and the super-normal had clashed together, fighting each other for space in my reality, they had fallen together in synergy. I felt in control now. It felt … right.

Slowly, perfectly, I allowed the furniture and objects to sink gently back to where they'd started. The thrumming noise faded, the thickness in the air lifted.

We could have stood there hours for all I know. Quiet. Awestruck. I felt … different. Somehow complete. Like I'd just taken a deep breath and exhaled. I sat on the bed, suddenly very tired.

Finally, Ellie spoke quietly. 'You know, I can't think how you must feel, Josh. I've tried to put myself in your place, but I really don't know what it must be like. All I know is that I'm frightened for you. Call me selfish, but you're my best friend, and you're fading away. I don't want to lose you.'

'What would *you* do, Ellie?' I replied, 'What would you do if you were given a chance like this? Would you ignore it and hope it goes away and just pray you don't cause a disaster the next time things get out of control? Or would you try and harness it, so that one day you might be able to do something amazing?'

'But look at you, Josh. What's the point of half-killing yourself in the hope you might one day do something amazing with these abilities? What's the point of wanting to save the world, if you're dead before you get the chance?'

'It's my life — my choice. What's one life compared to the lives of many?'

'It's *your* life, Josh. And it's a gift, so please don't throw it away.'

I felt so at peace right then. So calm. 'I've been given another gift, Ellie, something huge. I can't sit back and do nothing about it. Don't try and tell me you wouldn't do the same. If you were given the choice between saving yourself and saving the world, you'd save the world, every time.'

'There are other ways to be a hero, Josh.' She said. 'The world always needs saving, you know — it just seems like a big job for just one person.'

'You have to start somewhere.' I said.

She gave up arguing with me. I'm a stubborn fucker sometimes. Mum says I get it from her.


ELLIE:

You know, I remember that morning in July so clearly. It was my birthday, and Josh was taking me in to town to do some shopping. We decided to go in early so we could get done and nab a decent spot in one of the parks for the rest of the day. I couldn't quite believe he'd dragged his bony arse out of bed so early, but there we were, heading into town on a packed tube train in the morning rush hour.

He told me he'd been 'practising' a lot. I told him he looked thin.

It was a little before nine o'clock, and we had just left Kings Cross on the Piccadilly line when the bomb went off.

The reports say the train was only five hundred yards from the station. That's where it was found, at least. I know that line like the back of my hand, you know, and I can tell you we were a lot further into the tunnel than that.

We were in the second carriage, near the back when he turned to me and said, 'Something's wrong.'

Don't ask me how he knew. Maybe he'd developed some sort of Spidey-sense by this point, but he shot out of his seat and planted himself in the middle of that carriage just as the far end of it exploded.

The train rocked, people screamed as they were tossed like rubbish. I went flying into the people sitting opposite me. I righted myself and saw him standing there in the middle of the gangway with this visible, but at the same time unearthly energy coming from his hands. It was clear and rippling — almost glasslike — but not solid, know what I mean? And it had wrapped a perfect, terrifying, sphere around the explosion, trapping it before it had torn the carriage apart.

The lights went out and chaos found us. Screaming commuters trampled over each other in their panic, the air was saturated with smoke. I managed to pull myself to my feet and snatch hold of one of the ceiling straps.

Something hit me in the face, I don't know what, but I barely registered my broken nose, or the blood dribbling from it. I was coughing and covered my mouth with my sleeve so I could breathe more normally. The number of people in the carriage seemed to have tripled — at least that's what it felt like, you know? There were bodies everywhere — some moving, some not. I squinted and tried to fight my way through the pandemonium to get to Josh.

He was — with visible effort — pushing his hands closer together, compressing the flowing liquid-glass sphere and the vicious fireball inside, squeezing the life out of it. He was bathed in the light from the inferno he held captive, but more than that, he himself seemed to radiate his own light, you know? Like it was coming from within him. The air was thick with noise, all underpinned by a thrumming vibrating sound, like a jet plane flying too low, but I could hear his voice with perfect clarity above the din.

'I don't know what's going to happen when I let go!' He cried.

'Josh, just … *please!*' I yelled back, trailing off into a croak, trying to say a thousand things at the same time — I love you, don't leave me, help, I don't want to die, I don't want *you* to die — but I was hollowed out with fear and empty of words — know what I mean?

'Get out! Just get everyone out! I can't contain it!'

I looked at him helplessly, tears mixing in with the blood and dirt on my face and he bellowed 'ELLIE! GO! NOW!'

As I span round, I glimpsed his arms faltering and I heard a loud CRACK as a shockwave knocked me off my feet and shot me towards the back of the carriage. I hit my head and blacked out.

I don't know how long I was laying there; I came around to the sound of a deafening hum. The carriage lurched and gave a terrible screech. Metal shrieked on metal as the train was dragged back along in the direction it had come. I tried to see properly, but the blood from the cut on my forehead had got in my eyes and had turned everything pink and blurry, my nose was pulp and I could only breathe through my mouth. I was aware that Josh was no longer in the carriage and my last thought before unconsciousness swallowed me was: *how is the train moving?*

They found him on the tracks about a hundred metres into the tunnel. He never regained consciousness. I went to visit him every day in hospital, hoping I'd walk in and he'd be awake, but he never was. He just got thinner and paler, and despite doctors starting him on antiretroviral therapy, his CD4 continued to drop daily, until he had no immune system left. He died of pneumonia three weeks later. It was like using his ability so heavily had drained the life out of him — know what I mean? I suppose the virus just took over.

It stunned me at first that nobody questioned how the train ended up almost back where it started in King's Cross, helping those inside to get to safety quicker, or why the explosion didn't do more damage.

Some people said they'd felt the carriage moving. Others either didn't remember or chose to forget. Eyewitness accounts of that day were all conflicting anyway. It's not surprising when you think about it. When you're trapped deep underground in a smoke-filled train, terrified you're not getting out alive, your mind can play tricks on you.

I gave my own edited version of events, my head wound supporting my claim that I'd been knocked unconscious when the blast hit and I didn't remember a thing. Of course I didn't tell them there was more than one explosion in the carriage that day.

Experts said the Piccadilly Line explosion had a different pattern to the others. Press and the public were told that this was due to the tunnels being single-tracks with only a fifteen centimetre clearance around the edges for the train to pass through. This confined space reflected the force of the explosion back into the carriage and concentrated it in a tiny area.

I didn't bother to correct them.

That was five years ago now. It's taken me this long to feel ready to talk about what happened. I'd like to say writing it all down gives me some sort of closure, but even after all this time I still I have more questions than answers, know what I mean? It's my responsibility, though — to finish his story. I feel I owe him that much, at least.

I've rented a safe deposit box, and I'll put this document in it, along with some videos he made of his practice sessions. Maybe one day I'll be ready to share his story with the world. Not yet though.

I'll remember July 7, 2005 for three reasons: The first because it was my eighteenth birthday, the second because it was the day terrorists attacked London.

The third, because it was the day my best friend became a hero.

# MALICHI

# MALICHI

## THE ALBERT KENNEDY TRUST

I was born in Bangladesh. My father is from Pakistan and my mother is Bengali. I identify myself as an Asian gay Muslim.

I moved here when I was 12. I had very traumatic childhood. I was always getting beaten up by my dad. He's very religious. He's an Imam. It wasn't because of my sexuality, because I didn't know I was gay then and it isn't something people talk about. My family knew I was girly but people in Bangladesh are in denial about these things

I came here to King's Cross to live with my cousin. I was still a young child. I should have been living with my parents but I wasn't. I was living with people I didn't know. My cousin's wife wasn't very accepting of me. She thought I was a burden. So it was very hard for me.

I was 15 at the time and just before I did my GCSEs, they kicked me out of the house. Actually I was kicked out twice. The second time it happened the school called social services. I was fostered in Kingsbury. It was a very nice experience. My foster parents were Ethiopian, and very Christian. I was very proud of myself because I didn't have any problem whatsoever. I was an Asian Muslim living with African Christians, and I never had any problems. To me, we're all human beings, and they were very accepting of me and my culture and my religion.

My foster parents are the ones who treated me the way I should be treated, so I call them my mum and dad. They had two children of their own. The eldest moved out, so then I was the oldest. And then they fostered some other children. Before me, they only ever fostered Ethiopian children. But I was a good experience for them. I think I must have been a revelation for them, because after me they fostered children from other parts of the world.

My life is full of drama. I could make a film. Now I can laugh about it, but there was a time when I used cry about it. I tried to commit suicide twice. One time when I was back home, and one time when I was living with my cousin. I just wanted to die. My mum was always very nice to me but my dad was abusive. He used to beat me and my mum. I was the only child, and the only reason I'm here now is because of my mum. She sent me away for my own protection. Everything came to a head when my dad tried to sell me to a man who lived in Dubai. He wanted money. My dad stopped me from going to school and made me go to work. My mum couldn't do anything about it. We were a poor family from a rough area, and life was hard for her.

Alongside that, from the age of seven to the age of twelve I was used sexually. There were different people, but the worst was my blood cousin. He was about 30, old enough to be my dad, and he used to rape me basically. I hate him so much for using me. He took advantage of my vulnerability, and he blackmailed me and stuff like that. He told me that if I told anyone my life would be over. I didn't understand what was happening to me. At the time, I didn't know what sex was. We didn't have any sex education. I didn't go to school. I didn't even know what gay was. I didn't know what it was, but I used to do it because he got me into it.

I didn't think about until I was 17, in my first year of therapy, and we were doing sexual health. I went to see the nurse and I told her I might be at risk of an STD. She asked me why. It took me about ten minutes before I could tell her. In general I find it hard to sleep, especially in the summer. But that night I didn't sleep all night. I felt terrible. I felt anxious. I felt guilty. I felt that my life was useless. I thought I had no value anymore because I'd been used by someone for five years. I'd never really thought about it before. I was too busy with my housing and my education. I was a very nerdy student, and very fat. People used to pick on me because I was fat and call me names.

But one thing I must say, going through all these things has made me a strong person. I'm like a rock. If anyone kicks me, it doesn't hurt me as much. I used to cry every night but you see me now and I'm very confident. I'm slimmer now, and I like fashion. I love Lady Gaga. I have massive poster of her in my bedroom. I'm more outgoing now.

I've been seeing a counsellor for five years. And I do believe in God. I do believe in Allah. And I thank Allah for making this possible, for being who I am right now. I see life from many different aspects now. And I think life is beautiful. There is so much more to life, and so much more to do. I always wanted to be the flower who makes people smile. I appreciate life more now than I used to. I think the more you suffer in life, the more you learn and the more you grow, until you're ready for anything.

# INDEX OF CONTRIBUTORS

## DAVID LLEWELLYN

David Llewellyn was born in Pontypool in 1978. He is the author of five novels, including *Eleven*, *Everything Is Sinister* and *Doctor Who: Night Of The Humans*. He lives in Cardiff.

## JOE STOREY-SCOTT

Joe Storey-Scott is an artist who works in photography, text, paint, film and video. He has exhibited work in Edinburgh, Glasgow, London and his film *Mega Low Mania* has travelled to several international film festivals. He likes to keep his options open.

twentystorey.blogspot.com

## KEITH JARRET

Keith Jarrett lives and works in London. He is a regular on the performance poetry circuit, performing in both English and Spanish, and is the current London and UK Farrago Poetry Slam Champion. In February 2010, Keith won the Untold London 'Write Queer' prize for short fiction. He also facilitates a literacy project and mentors young people. Keith is now working on his first novel, set in a Pentecostal church.

### KRISTIAN JOHNS

Kristian Johns always had a love of words; he picked up his first book at the age of two and never looked back. He is a regular contributor to *QX Magazine*, runs a successful blog and corrects other people's grammar as an editor for RBI. In his spare time he enjoys rock music, drinking too much coffee and watching superhero films.

sexdrugssausagerolls.wordpress.com

### NORTH MORGAN

North Morgan is a suited wage-slave by day and a topless Nietzschean clubber also by day, and night. He has received around 1,100,000 hits on his blog, which converted into four stalkers, none of whom have yet murdered him. North Morgan hides in London.

londonpreppy.blogspot.com

### PAUL BURSTON

His books include the critically acclaimed novels *Shameless* (shortlisted for the State of Britain Award 2001), *Star People* and *Lovers & Losers* (shortlisted for the Stonewall Award 2007). His latest novel is *The Gay Divorcee*. He also hosts 'London's peerless gay literary salon' Polari and is a curator at the London Literature Festival.

paulburston.com

# BOYS & GIRLS

THE
NEXT
BEST
THING

# CONTENTS

# BOYS & GIRLS

### Edited by Paul Burston

GLASSHOUSE
B O O K S

ISBN 9781907536090

# THE NEXT BEST THING

## KAREN MCLEOD

Cynthia pulls up with her bony nose.

'Hello Cynthia,' I say, crouching down to look at her clavicles. It is a thrill to say her name, all adult as if we are meeting in a discotheque. Cynthia – the name hits your tongue and melts like spray-can cream.

Glancing out the car window, she gives me one cool look taking in my clothes, my peach earrings with matching necklace. They were good when I left the house, but standing here they are not. She stares at the hat on my head. I have worn this to hide the haircut she gave me on Thursday. The style has been named twice at school, first the acorn cup, then Joan of Arc in English. I had asked for a feathered bob.

'Hello. Do you still like your hair?' she says, holding the steering wheel with her leather driving gloves.

'Lovely. I mean thank you. I bought the mousse you suggested,' I say, pulling off the purple hat and ruffling it. I know she is thinking my face is too big, not that my hair is too small.

'It always takes a while to grow into the style,' she says.

Flo gets out and slams the car door. She has a feathered bob that took no time to grow into the style. She walks up tight-lipped with her eye balls looking up and over in their sockets. It is one of those looks which say: I have a story for you, you won't believe this one, what she's done now.

Our friendship is full of these episodes, full of Cynthia and tales of twisted punishments.

'Six o'clock, Florence. You know what I told you,' Flo's mother says.

Her window goes up electrically and seals the car. Cynthia disappears. We see ourselves and the train station sign behind us. I can smell their family smell on Flo's rucksack, new carpet mixed with new Dad. I kept my rucksack in my room so it didn't absorb the deposits of moulting dog and distilled casserole. The rucksacks were bought for today. It was my idea to get them. They correspond, one canary yellow with orange trim and the other satsuma orange with yellow trim. The word Voyager is in quirky lettering on the Velcro flaps.

Sensible is the word. Before being allowed out without an adult I had to promise to be this as Flo can't ever be this again; not after the shoplifting incident in HMV. I am kitted out for the role: Dad's *A to Z*, cartons of tropical juice, peppermints and emergency phone call change (to be kept separate in my purse).

London Town is at the end of the train line. We call it a Town to make it smaller in our minds and less like the never-ending maze of alleys and sex, which it is. One reason for me begging to go is because Sophie with the horse teeth came back from her holidays with her school jumper flung over her shoulders and said 'Italian girls hold hands all the time in public'. Sophie had tried to start a trend by striding like the Pied Piper round the playground holding Donna's hand, but the fashion never became one because of jeering from the chip-shop gang. Sophie said girls holding hands was normal over there, meaning it wasn't over here, which I found out for myself.

In summer, London Town is full of such foreigners with their bright rucksacks and packed lunches. They even make it to the outskirts where me and Flo live. Each season they flock to the language school by the local baths like disorientated parrots. You can see them outside Woolworths – which must seem exotic to them – turning round the map of the roads, making here sound like somewhere else with their strange pronunciations.

There is this thing called a *Capital Card* they've brought out which costs eighty pence. You can roam as far as you like all day on the buses, tubes and trains, even go out the other side of London up north. Not that I expect we will go very far, Flo says visiting Pizza Hut and Top Shop by Charing Cross station will probably be all the London we need for one day. In her fourteen years she's already been to Pizza Hut twice with her Dad (who we all know tries to buy her love with badges) and sampled a slice and a refillable bowl with bacon bits from the salad bar.

The train turns out to be one of those disappearing British Rail ones with the hard to twist handles. A man reaches out and does the mechanism for us. We go far down the carriage in case the man expects something for helping. We find the closed buffet car and sit in the green bristle-velvet seats pretending to be rich ladies who pull each other's hair on Wednesday night TV.

An ashtray is stuck on the table between us.

'So what happened?' I say.

'She found my diary again. She nearly didn't let me come out with you,' she says, igniting a pencil with an imaginary lighter.

'Oh. Why?' I say, smoking an invisible slim panatela.

'I don't know, because she's a bitch? She always reads it, so, I decided to

write a whole lot of lies to confuse her.' Flo has the same expressions as her mother, critical blue eyes and a restless way of twisting her blonde hair into a tight coil round her finger.

'What like? What did you write about us?'

'Oh nothing about that! I just said something a bit like,' Flo looks out the window. I follow her nose to see what she is seeing. A woman is washing her armpits with a flannel through an open bathroom window. Her shiny breasts make me look at my deck shoes. Then a woman has pegged out her lacy nightie on a whirligig and turns it to catch the breeze.

'Every morning they must wait for the train to expose themselves,' she says, 'They must be so bored.'

'What did you write then?' I say.

There is no one else in the buffet carriage. Flo jumps behind the bar and puts on a cockney accent and says, 'What's your poison, guvnor?' She tells me to watch the door as she looks through the shelves under the bar for anything good. I want to say stop, but I stop myself instead.

As we approach London Bridge we realise we have only ten minutes to practice our vocab. This is all part of the rucksack game, to pretend to be a foreign visitor up London Town. In order to save time we've divvied up the responsibilities of the Italian language: I've learnt *where is the station?* and Flo has learnt, *what is the soup of the day?*

Pizza Hut isn't open yet. Flo takes out a cigarette and lights it with a box of matches. She stands with her weight on one hip and blows into the crowds of walkers-by. Through the window a man with a red shirt and black trousers is folding napkins on the table and wiping wine glasses. I can see a tall menu standing up with pictures of bubbling cheese on pizzas and I

can't wait. I haven't ordered from a menu by myself before as I've only ever been to a Carvery, which was peculiar with its thick carpet, wooden panels and undercurrents of nursing homes.

When we come out of Top Shop Flo slips on a pair of big sunglasses.

'Flo,' I say. 'You didn't did you?' and she smiles and links my arm and pulls me away fast.

In Trafalgar Square we are in front of the lions. Children are climbing all over them. Pigeon mess is everywhere. I get out the *A to Z* and go to the page with the folded corner. Dad has drawn in red felt tip a one centimetre circle around the dot of Charing Cross. This is the area he said we should stick to and not go any further, especially not off the page.

'The map is so small Nelson's column isn't even on it,' I say.

'Where?' Flo says, looking at my finger.

'Can't you forget the bloody map?' she says, turning away.

'What?' I say.

'We can do what we like. No one is watching us.'

From her pocket Flo pulls out another pair of sunglasses and unfolds the arms and slots them onto my face.

'There,' she says. 'Now we look the same.' I see her Technicolor face, her glorious flicks.

Beside a fountain we spot a party of dark-haired foreign looking teenagers. They have pigeons on their heads.

'Do you want to feed the birds?' I say.

'No,' she says.

'It's what you do when you come here. It's bad luck if you don't,' I say.

'It's bad luck if they shit on your head,' she says.

'Let's go over here. We should start speaking foreign or we won't do it,' I say, pointing towards a large group.

'OK,' Flo says looking around. I go and stand near the girls who are speaking something fast, I think it may be Italian, but it could be Spanish. They are all wearing rucksacks like ours but have woollen Benetton jumpers in greens and pinks and oranges. Flo makes a face like they are all spastics. I reach out to grab her hand, like Sophie talked about, but she has it in her anorak pocket. The students sense us and walk off, reforming near a fountain. The space on the floor is filled immediately with grey pecking birds. I can see we don't appear the same as the students, even with our bags nearly identical to theirs and our sunglasses the latest model. I suddenly wish we had come as ourselves, in our jeans. The three quarter length chinos I have on are a little tight around my bottom in an English way.

'Look there's a gallery. Let's go into the gift shop, I bet they have good badges and pencils,' Flo says.

'Alright, but we have enough money to buy something if we want it,' I say to her back.

We walk into the National Gallery through the revolving doors and the security man points to a table. Other people are opening their bags to reveal what's in them. The stolen sunglasses are in mine and I open the bag as if it's my mouth at the dentist, just a fraction. The man gets hold of my bag and has a good look which I take personally. I hold my breath until I'm arrested.

'Fine,' the man says, handing it back, beckoning two fingers at the queue behind me. I am not arrested.

'Look at these.' Flo is standing by a plastic tub full of coloured gonks; stupid fiery headed plastic monsters which fit on pencil tops.

'They are nice,' I say.

I go over to the postcards. There is a black and white one of a woman with a hard fringe and a black shiny bob. She reminds me of Cynthia so I pick it up and examine it, then go to the desk to pay. It costs ten pence which seems a lot to spend in one go but I am pleased as I get a free paper bag with a perforated edge plus the pillars of the gallery are on the front.

When I go back to the gonks to find Flo she isn't there. I stand and look around at the people browsing books with naked statues on the front. It's as quiet as a library.

I wait by the revolving door for fifteen minutes watching people kiss each other on their cheeks hello twice.

In the phone box I call home.

'Seven seven eight Oh eight four one?'

'Hello mum?' I say.

'Hold on. Yes, I said put it over by the bureau, didn't I? Sorry about that. Are you having a nice time up there?'

'Flo's gone missing,' I say.

'What? Where are you? Where did you see her last?' Mum says.

'We were in the gift shop of the museum over there. I bought a postcard and turned around and she'd gone,' I say.

'Well. Have you looked for her?'

'Of course I have. I don't know where else she might be. I've stayed within the circle.'

'Good, don't go outside of Dad's map. Well, just retrace your steps and if you can't find her, ask a policeman,' she says.

13

***

I order my pizza. I sit looking out the window for Flo. The sun is ridiculous and bright drying the pavement. My head nods up every time the door opens. The umbrella is wet on the carpet splayed out like an exhausted lettuce. I look at the map of the area in the *A to Z*, then the map outside the area. The maps all lead into other maps on other pages, up down left and right. I find home on page one two five. The waiter keeps coming up and asking if everything is alright and I know he wants me to leave.

Cynthia's black car is out the front of the station when I come down the stairs.

'Where is she?' she says.

'I don't know,' I say. 'We were in the gallery. There were so many people. I waited for four hours,' I say, no words making up for my fault.

'What did you make her do?' she says. 'She told me all about the Italian you've been practicing. I'm going home to phone the police.'

The car pulls off. I walk home.

When I get back I look out my bedroom window from the eleventh floor. I can see the black car is there at the top of the road, parked outside Cynthia's house. I unpack my bag; inside are the sunglasses, the map, a pizza box with half a cheese and tomato deep pan. The grease has seeped through the box and onto the rucksack.

The phone rings. It's Flo for me.

'I'm home,' she says. 'My mum's said I'm not to go up to London with you anymore,' she says.

'Why? Where did you go?' I say. 'I waited in Pizza Hut for three hours.'

'I can't tell you now,' Flo says. Then the phone goes dead. I go back to my room and look at the postcard in the light of the window.

A bob is a hair cut to be desired.

# JAIL
# BAIT

# JAIL BAIT

## STELLA DUFFY

Jill's telling me the girl unit at Holloway is the coolest thing she's ever heard of. Special and new made and all shiny and clean. And just for us. It was on the radio – I didn't hear it, I don't listen to that kind of radio, don't listen to any kind of radio, got enough voices of my own to listen to, tell the truth – but Jill heard about it and she told me and we thought it was just so cool. It's not got any of the old cows in it, sad old slags and the slappers who've been around forever anyway and don't know where else to be, except just this side of north London, downwind of Hampstead, turn back if you get to Arsenal, you've gone too far. You've always got to go too far.

Getting our first tattoos together. Real tattoos, paid for and sterile and everything. Watching the man painting on her skin, soft flesh raised into hoarse red welts, wiping away the blood and adding new colour, pretty yellow and blue and deep red darker than her blood. Then my turn and Jill said it wouldn't hurt, didn't hurt her, did it? She wasn't whimpering for fuck's sake. So I took off my bra, lay down, heart shape over heart space. But it did hurt. Too damn much. I made him stop even though she said I couldn't. Made him give up halfway through. He said I must have a low pain threshold. Maybe I do. I also have a tattoo of a broken heart.

Sitting in Jill's bedroom – also kitchen, lounge, bathroom, the lot – sitting on the floor, leaning against her knees, hoping if I wait here long enough she might stroke my head again, play with my hair. She doesn't. We're sitting there and then she says how fucking crap the end of daylight saving is, how she can't stand it and now the bloody sun's coming in waking her at eight in the morning and then it's dark by four, dark before the day's even started and too damn cold and what the fuck are we supposed to do for Christmas dinner anyway? I thought it was a big leap from the end of October to the full stuffed turkey, flaming Christmas pudding, but you could see what she meant. Then she said we should go to Holloway. For the festive season. And I'm like fuck me but you're a mad cunt, madder than I am, and Jill says that's just not possible, just not possible. But she's not making a whole lot of sense either, she can't mean it, that place stinks and anyway last time we tried that shit she got to Holloway, I ended up in bloody Styal, two weeks out of my mind in boredom valley and then luckily just about loopy enough to get shunted off to community care hole. Left there in a halfway house to nowhere, easily influenced, just keep the mad bitch on the medication and she'll be good as gold, good as Goldilocks, steal your fucking porridge you stupid great cunts and what do you mean I can't see her, I have to see her, who else is there? Then fuck you bitch and now what's the problem, you've got another eye haven't you? Oh Christ and such a lot of blood and God I hope it's not mine, there's nothing like an institutionalised period to start the day, end the day, start the week – more radio fucking shite – and then the quiet and the sweet icecream and jellies, temazepam baby I am, will be, ever be, hush now good girl.

Anyway, anyway, the point being that the last time we tried to come in from the cold they tore us apart and broke my heart and Jill came tumbling

after. But apparently . . . Holloway's got this new young offenders unit and the radio lady from the north thinks that's shit, thinks all the money will go there, showcase for the dangerous young ones, too much of a good thing and what about the poor little girls in the frozen north, where will all their good money go? Stay down here baby, warm in the soft south where it always has been, did you not notice it's why we moved here too? So – it's the end of October. We just have to do it well enough, big but not too big, within the next couple of weeks, then the least it'll be is remand and maybe even a few months more to get us all the way into spring, fever of the recently freed.

But we have to do it right. Too big and we'll not see summer soon enough. Too small and it's a crap cell night, maybe a caution, and worse than that the possibility of another fucking year fucking the carers. So whoring's out because that's always leading back to some foster daddy, let me hold you and make it all better baby, oh yes please do, that's just what I need. And shoplifting's good for the clothes, or your dinner, or even just the sheer fucking thrill of being bad in the shining light of security cameras and in the face of Henry Stupid the thick bastard who stands at the door pretending to be a security guard, biceps for brains and a dick the size of my clit, but shoplifting won't get us Christmas crackers with plastic scissors inside. And housebreaking is possible but Jill's still terrified of dogs and gets tinnitus with too much loud noise – or a too hard smack on the head – and if we want them to get us it would have to be dog or alarm and what's the point of the pointless break-in if you get away with it? Indeed.

First break-in. We were thirteen, fourteen at the most. Maybe Jill was already fourteen. Fast shared a gram of speed and running around the town, new town with walkways turned into airplane runaways, ready to take off there was so much of the too-much energy spilling round my veins. Then Jill says we should use the excess and do a job. She's been watching daytime re-runs of *The Sweeney*, it takes me a minute to work out what she's talking about. There's a place on the corner, a flat above the closed off-licence, the woman who lives there works every day, gets the bus first thing and isn't back until dark. She'll be safely at the office. It's easy to get in. No dog, no alarm, she's probably not even thirty yet that woman, no money for any good security shit. Good guess, no security at all, but she's got a great place. Easy in through the back window and it's nice in there. Just bedroom and lounge, kitchen and bathroom. And all of it girlie soft and warm, too much pink, but it'll do us. We eat bacon and eggs – Jill can't eat much, but speed's never really affected my appetite, I'm weird like that. I can just soak those drugs right up. She does me a big breakfast – half a packet of bacon, three eggs just how I like them, yolk running all over the bacon, bright yellow into the setting fat, geography rivulets on the plate. Bacon's a bit too salty, smoked back, but good anyway. I chew the rind and walk through the little flat. We think about a place like this, maybe Jill and I could get a place together, share it. The woman's got chocolates in her fridge, creme eggs too, we take the telly into the bedroom and get into bed, sheets quite clean, must have been changed only a few days ago and no fucking or period stains, maybe she's got a washing machine, easier that way to wash your sheets whenever you want to. We eat chocolate and watch telly, laugh at the phone-in moan-in, but then it's too comfortable and warm and we fall asleep and we've got problems of our own. It's dark, the only light is from

the telly, the woman's walked in and guess who's sleeping in her bed and she's off on one and screaming at us, hitting at us and I don't know what the fuck she's so pissed off for, we didn't take anything. Jill can't believe she's hitting her and I can't believe she's hitting Jill, can't she see how stupid that is? She's fucking lucky we fell asleep, we were going to take loads of shit and we didn't so what's the fucking problem? What is your fucking problem you stupid fucking ignorant bitch? Big dry cleaning bill I expect. Hard work getting all that blood off the pretty pink duvet in your basic home washing machine. The woman moved out weekend after that. Squatters moved in. Bet they didn't keep it as nice as she did.

Jill rolls a joint, mostly tobacco, thin rub of hash into it, then special treat for the goodest of good girls, sprinkling of coke across the top – she worked last night in the City boy street, sweet rich boys paying in kind. Kind City boy forced to hand over cash too when Jill explained what was going to happen when she stopped twisting his balls and the blood flooded back in and then out again when she used the blade hidden in her other hand. Fifty quid, just like that. Scared city boy pissing in his own wind. But driving home anyway. Whimpering back to his girl friend and just an especially difficult day in the money markets darling, I'm a bit tired, maybe I'll have a little lie down. No you bitch, don't fucking touch me there, I didn't mean that kind of a lie down, for fuck's sake, is that all you bloody women ever think about? Jill and I lie back and dream of Holloway, special shared room and painted walls and breakfast and lunch and dinner and hide out in the house of girlies until summer comes around. I'm wondering, just briefly, if Jill's got this completely right, if it's all going to be so lovely, I mean the point is, it is a house of detention right? But she's sure it must be great

because otherwise why would the Tory bitch on the radio be so concerned and anyway, even if it's just like the same old place, no new paint job or anything, if it isn't for the old ones, if it's just for us, then think of how it will be, no old lady smells and no mad mothers crying for their fostered babies and the following, always following because we're always the little ones. We'll be big girls, just us, our very own home from home. Which, when the home you're homing from is ten foot square of peeling damp and the screams of the dozy cunt next door who will keep welcoming him into her bed and then getting surprised when she finds his fist into her face as well, if that's home and Jack Frost is on his way, then maybe anything's better. Or maybe I just wanted Jill to stroke my hair again. Like she did. Just the once. Soft stroking like she meant it, not absent action like I might have been the cat or her own head in need of a good itch. Anyway, anyway, the hash is spreading my mind all over the place, it's chocolate spread brain, and then because neither of us smokes tobacco if we can help it, we're getting a nicotine rush too and I'm just starting to refocus when the pretty little truth drug kicks in on top of all that and my poor bitch of a brain doesn't know what to do. Mouth opens and closes and doesn't know if it should laugh or talk and starts to say words, any will do, but tobacco dries my lips and nothing comes out just a goo gah of bollocks and pretty soon Jill thinks I'm really funny, really fucking funny and I so want her not to laugh at me, I want that hand to stroke my head not point fucking laughing at me.

First time laughing, too stoned, new to us, first time laughing so much, giggling stoned laughter and it won't go away and I've peed my pants and Jill and me both just laughing even more at that, sticky ammonia turning cold in my jeans. She's trying to cut out a line of speed to sharpen me

up, take the edge off the giggle, but her hand's shaking so much and I'm laughing so much I blow it all over the table. Stopped me laughing though.

Nothing to stop her laughing at me now and I'm not wasting good drugs on her sense of humour this time. So I'm fucked off and hate her. Hate her hard. Worried by the hate, it's the one that scares me, and I really don't like to hate Jill, but she is so not going to stop laughing, she's having far too good a time and I think maybe I need to leave now, go out for a walk, get away from the laughing bitch because I might just have to smack her big mouth if she doesn't stop, and I've never hit Jill before, though she's hit me loads of times and I don't know if I could hit her, not really, but right now I might just slam my fist so far into that laughing gob of hers it'll come out her cunt next time she sees it. I don't like being this angry. Worries me. Don't like it at all. And then – bliss, sweet rapture, and praise the gifts of the virgin who'd hate to see me harm a hair on the beloved's head, I've slammed pissed off hands hard into my pocket and there's a couple of jellies in there with the condoms and the polo mints. I know, but it only sounds like an odd combination at first. You figure it out. And then maybe I can just about do this. The jellies and the coke and the hash? I don't know if it's a great combination, it's not quite the real thing, but fuck it I might as well anyway because daylight saving has all gone and it's dark at four thirty now and so we're not going anywhere, right? Wrong.

Jill stops laughing and pulls me out of the door with her. I don't need a coat she says, even though it's bloody freezing, shit sleety rain far too early in November and slashing at my face, but she tells me not to worry, there's a nice warm BMW parked just around the corner and we can put the heater

on full and move in for half an hour or so. Jill can't drive but she knows everything else there is to know about cars. How to get through the electric locking system. How to turn off the alarm without a key. How to start the motor. Jill fucked a mechanic for a few months last year, stole his knowledge and fucked off with his new set of tools too. Left his dick, not the best of his tools. And it's a nice car, big and easy to drive. At least it is until Jill starts trying to direct me, over there, that right turn, no not this, the next one, shit you've missed it, u-turn, here, yes of course you can, you fucking well can, don't talk shit, you fucking well can. Fucking well can't. Coke, hash and jellies, power steering power steered from the passenger seat. Straight into an oncoming Nissan. We barely move, the BMW takes the swipe with a fat and solid crunch – side impact bars, air bags as standard, there's something about these company cars that makes even facing the wrong way in rush hour not seem so bad. The tinny little Japanese spins out and then back into the line of traffic, driver looks as if he thinks it might be all right. He's facing the right way. His neck isn't broken. Chassis is though. I'm dazed and Jill's pulling at my hand, grabs me out of my seat and we're running fast, down a couple of dark streets, through a pathway, old lady shrinking against the wall, holding her trolley to her like a shield, thanking God we weren't interested. A couple of people chase at first, but they don't really care. Much more concerned about the guy in the Nissan than the couple of girls who've pinched some rich git's car. God knows he'll have enough insurance. I bet Nissan Man's only third party, he looks like a local. Want to tell Jill, but she'll hate me for worrying, looking back. Jill doesn't look back. Quick turn left, no idea of exactly where we're headed but we know there's a canal along here somewhere, no-one comes to a canal at dusk. Not unless they're running too. Into an overgrown estate and thanking winter

now, glad of early sunset. I'm fretting about fingerprints but Jill is so sure that's irrelevant, bloke'll get his car back and don't the cops have better to think about than that and who the fuck knows where we live anyway? No-one. No-one but Jill. We find the canal and follow the line down towards town, brighter lights and I really am freezing now, coke rush long gone, just a headache from too many drugs and the adrenaline mix, temples throbbing, I'm thinking maybe we're headed home, maybe we can leave it for tonight, back to Jill's and a bag of chips, vinegar and grease on my hands until the morning, but Jill sees me shivering and my goose-pimpled skin takes her ahead to the turkey. She wants us safe and warm for Christmas. Tucked up cosy and waiting for Santa. Inside.

First Christmas alone. The mother and father have gone away. Packed their car with a DNA-variegation of children and driven to their cousins in the north. And I will not go with them. I will not go to the happy family and play the good child. We have been fighting for weeks and then she said it, the mother, ok, don't come, we'll take the others. You stay here. By yourself. That's fine. She turned the electricity off as she left and removed the key card. Christmas morning listening to the one radio in the house that had batteries and boiling milk for hot Weetabix, grateful for the gas stove. I'm eleven, Jill's twelve and a half. She knocks on the door, shivering in pyjamas and dressing gown. Her lot are still asleep and can she watch telly at my place, she knows we have too many kids here for them to attempt the sort of tv rules they have at her house. No tv. Jill can't believe it, is shocked – all alone? Stunned – they really left you all alone? And so fucking excited. Stays all morning. By eleven we've finished the Baileys and started on the Tia Maria. Weetabix with hot milk and whiskey. Her Gran swears

by whiskey to keep you well, milk to line the stomach, makes Jill a hot toddy every night in winter. Jill says it will stop us getting sick. It doesn't, but we're not bothered. *Morecombe and Wise* are probably on telly now, it doesn't matter. Queen's Message comes and goes and Jill still isn't going home, she's having too much fun and I do think, I really do, that maybe her Gran will be worried, but then the thought passes and anyway, she won't know to find Jill here, thinks my lot are all away. They are. Early evening and there's Advocaat and some cheery cherry brandy and Jill thinks we should set fire to a pudding. But we haven't got a Christmas pudding, so it's the last of the Weetabix and a third of a bottle goes on top, because there's alcohol in Christmas pudding too, isn't there? So it can't matter how much we throw on. Can't matter until the lit Weetabix flies up to the greasy nets and we've left the gas on to heat the place and there's a lot of flame, lot of fire and we run out to the balcony, Jill screaming, nylon dressing gowns glowing in the night wind. Hospital, new homes, new parents, Jill's Gran can't cope and she joins me in care limbo.

Until that Christmas Jill had only been my best friend. After that she was my only friend.

We're out now, so we may as well stay out. We may as well make it happen tonight. That's Jill's plan. Along the canal for a bit, past a couple of girls out working. Not looking for work, actually working. Jill gives a few pointers to the one giving a blow job.

'Slower love, slower. The gentle gobble's what the bloke's after, aren't you mate?'

Punter and girl look up, Jill's smiling, as much as you can smile with your gob wide open miming the mouthing. The girl slows down, the

punter nods relief and grins, winks at Jill. The kid's probably only about fourteen, no fucking idea yet.

'That's it love. You've got him now. He's happy now. well done love, that's it, keep on, good girl.'

The bloke's smiling, eyes closed, pants down. Jill reaches for his wallet, poking out of his trouser pocket, grabs a twenty for herself and pushes another into the girl's bra top. Poor bitch must be freezing. All the while Jill's sweet talking the pair of them through it.

'Now you've got it, good girl, that's the way. Soft and slow. See love, there's some things your mum'll never teach you.'

He's grinning and moaning to himself and the girl's sucking and slobbering for all she's worth, eyes wide and delighted.

We walk on, maybe ten yards and once we're almost at the bridge Jill shouts out, 'That's it! Good girl. You're doing a great job, great job. Soft and slow and get them going and now—'

The girl looks up, mouth full, the punter opens his smiling eyes, grateful inquisitive looks towards the pair of us from both of them, 'Now bite the fucker off!'

Jill screams with delight, girl chokes with laughter, man freaks, cock shrivels, nothing to blow. God knows why they do it, men are a fuck of a lot braver than us. I'd never trust anything that tender to the teeth of a stranger. We run off and Jill can't get over herself, fucking delighted she is. Twenty quid richer too.


First trick. Jill's idea. We've both done it, Jill figures we might as well start getting paid for it. Jill figures. I'm fifteen, she's sixteen. Legal. Real. I'm nervous about it though so she tells me to watch her, see how she goes

and if she can do it, then so can I. A fuck's a fuck, right? And I can just stop with a blow job if I really want to. I don't know. Seems to me your actual fuck – eyes closed, all noise and panting – is a damn sight less personal than having some stranger's dick in my mouth. Anyway, she's street-cornering herself and I'm stopping in the dark part, under the arches, watching her, and these lads come up. It's a stag party. They want her for the groom. What'll she do for twenty quid? We didn't know much about market forces at the time. She offered the lot. Quite a show, best man got a handjob, bride's little brother got a blowjob, and then Jill's feeling a bit knackered so she calls me out of the corner and asks the groom how does he fancy me and her together? This is all out in the fucking street, mind. Anyway, course he does. So I'm there right and Jill reckons it'll be fine and then we're fooling about and now the groom's got his dick out and Jill reckons I should do him, get it over with, at least she's there with me. So I turn to do him and then I see it's all of them that are waiting. Not just the groom and this wasn't the deal and Jill's saying no, this wasn't the deal, but that's not the fucking point, right? The best man's not quite so drunk now. She did half a dozen of them and I did six of the others. This was not voluntary. Except when they left the little brother ran back and gave us another twenty each. So it wasn't really rape either. Was it? We got better at it after that. More fucking careful anyway.

So I'm thinking about that girl and how I'm so bloody happy to be running round winter with Jill and not on my knees by the canal and we're coming back up to Holloway Road now and Jill says that's auspicious. It's a sign. Yeah, it's a fucking road sign. Not what she means. And there's lights and cars and a few drunks and some young people in groups, pissed and

laughing on their way out for the night, and Jill's speeding now, really fucking speeding, God knows what on. Cold and potential and the twenty quid in her pocket I guess. And she's looking all around and thinking who can we do? What can we do? Then she sees it, other side of the road, furniture shop. And in the window, a bloody fairy tale bed. Really fairy tale. A four poster straight out of *Sleeping Beauty*. All over girlie shit and frills and pretty and embroidered roses, wide curtains with white flounces and I can't believe that Jill even thinks that looks like anything, but she's just completely taken with it, and they've done some special lighting on it too, it's all soft and golden, glowing in the cold street. And the cover turned down and a silk nightie laid out just waiting for the Princess to float in and sleep forever, no night dancing to wear out her shoes, no hidden pea to bruise her delicate skin. Perfect.

And then Jill's got a rubbish bin and it just goes right through the window, before I can say not to, before I can even ask what the fuck she's doing and the glass only takes two hits and then it shatters, glass mountain collapses with sparkling prisms all around us, glitter snow on the ground and the ringing of alarm bells. And Jill just takes her time, gives me her clothes, one by one, like I'm the fucking palace maid and I fold them up and put them on the ground because what else can I do and then she's naked and she climbs in through the broken window, glass under her feet but that doesn't matter and I help her put on the nightie and she just gets into bed. Climbs into the bed. I plump up the pillows and tuck her in and kiss her goodnight, pull the curtains around her. I'd turn out the lights but they're flashing blue.

First night in the girl place. It's OK. Really it is. Lots better than I've been in before, that's for sure. It's really not bad. The lady on the radio was right.

I mean it is Holloway, but it is pretty flash too. Jill doesn't know though. It all took ages working out what had happened, if they were going to do her or section her. I was easy, accomplice, best friend, no nutter me. Not now. Only then they figured same for her – she was bad, not mad this time. True too. She's not mad. Pissed off but. Jill turned twenty while we were on remand, they reckoned she's too old for this. Too late for it to do her any good. Fucked her off no end. I didn't think it would be all right being here without her. But it's not that bad. Not as bad as I thought anyway.

Still, it'll be summer soon.

# KNITTING

# FOR

# BEGINNERS,

# 1960

# KNITTING FOR BEGINNERS, 1960

## VG LEE

At school everyone is pony mad although nobody, not even Joanna Bayliss the richest and most popular girl in our year, have their own pony or take riding lessons. Joanna and her two friends, Estelle and Lesley pretend to be horses in the playground. Joanna's horse is pure white and named Silver Star - Estelle and Lesley make do with a chestnut and a pinto. Nobody dares to be a black horse as that would annoy Linda Portman who is always Black Beauty and has a nasty temper if another horse tries to drink from the same puddle.

If Linda Portman didn't exist I'd have been a black stallion called Midnight. I'd gallop gracefully up to Joanna, nuzzle her two friends out of the way, and then together we'd gallop through the school gates our hooves striking fire off the rocky terrain.

Joanna Bayliss has a grown-up brother living in New York. He sends her broderie anglaise party dresses, also at least three angora boleros, a fun fur coat and a pair of red leather bootees with a small heel. Joanna's clothes never seem to get dirty. She isn't the kind of girl to have a leaky fountain pen and she isn't the kind of girl that boys flick their own leaky pens at.

On my last school report our form teacher Miss Wozencroft wrote 'Bonnie is a bright likable child who fails to concentrate', which isn't true. I concentrate very hard on Joanna; the length and darkness of her eyelashes, the curve of her cheek, her ringlets. Joanna tosses her ringlets

at least a dozen times in every lesson. I've counted, making a pencil mark in the margin of my exercise book. Her highest score for ringlet tossing is twenty-three. Then there are her surprisingly chubby wrists with the silver charm bracelets Miss Wozencroft confiscated but was forced to return after Joanna's mother wrote a letter of complaint to the school governor.

All around the playground is a low brick wall with iron railings set into it. There is a wooden bench where I sit and eat my sandwiches during the morning break. Usually I have the bench to myself but to my surprise one morning, Joanna sat down next to me and took her packed lunch from her shiny leather satchel. Sticking out of a side pocket was a recorder. I hadn't known Joanna played an instrument.

I said, 'Are you good at the recorder?'

'Not really,' she said, 'But mummy thinks it would be nice for me to accompany her on the piano at family parties.'

'I expect you come from a musical family?'

'No.'

Silently she ate her sandwiches.

'What's in your sandwiches?' I asked.

'Ham and pickle,' she said.

She didn't ask me what was in mine. At any moment she'd finish, pick up her satchel and leave me. I said, 'Do you want to play a game?'

She pulled a face, 'What sort of game?'

From my own satchel I took out a wooden ruler and pointed to her recorder, 'We run round the playground hitting the boys with these. Not hard but hard enough to get them to take notice. They'll chase us and try to kiss us.'

'Will they?' Joanna looked impressed.

'Yes,' I said firmly.

'Okay.'

We raced up to where a group of boys were playing cricket. I shouted 'Tally-ho' and was pleased when Joanna also shouted 'Tally-ho'. We poked and batted the boys in the ribs or their backs. 'Bet you can't catch me!' we cried. Together we ran across the playground, jumped onto the wall and clung to the railings. The boys did chase us. As we held on tightly they banged us on our shoulders before rushing back to their game. No boy actually tried to kiss us. I was quite glad about that and Joanna didn't seem bothered either.

In the afternoon break we played the same game and at the end of the day Joanna walked arm in arm with me to the school gates. Her mother was leaning against the open door of their two-tone Vauxhall Victor. Joanna waved and her mother waved back. Joanna turned to me. 'That was the best day's play I've ever had,' she said.

I bumped my face into hers and kissed her hard on the cheek, my nose hitting against her eyelid.

'Ouch!' she said laughing, 'You're a complete nutcase.'

Gran was late collecting me. I'm often the last one waiting at the school gate but I didn't mind. I was friends with the most popular girl in our year. I'd made up our play and she'd found it, 'the best'.

The next morning I couldn't wait to get to school. I kept telling gran not to dawdle whereas normally she kept telling me. As I came into the playground I saw Joanna, surrounded by her usual group of friends. She had her back to me but I knew she knew I'd arrived by the way everyone else looked at me and then at her.

'Hello Joanna,' I said.

Her head swung round, thick curls brushing my face and then she moved a step away. 'Mummy said I wasn't to play with you anymore,' she said, her expression quite friendly but as if she was speaking politely to someone she didn't like very much.

'But why?'

My face and ears felt boiling hot. The other girls stared at me, their eyes sharp with interest.

'Mummy said your game was most unladylike.'

'But you said you enjoyed it.'

'Not that much,' she answered, 'Anyone going to the canteen?'

They all were.

On Friday afternoons Miss Wozencroft teaches us Practical Work. We've learnt how to make a sailing boat and Nelson's tricorn hat out of several sheets of newspaper, how to cover our exercise books with jolly pictures taken from a pile of old magazines and the week after Joanna and I fell out, 'how to knit'.

Miss Wozencroft stood on the dais at the front of the class, 'Hands up all those who can knit?'

Only three children put up their hands.

'Well good gracious. At ten years old I could knit a raglan sleeved pullover,' she said, 'Our first project will be a hot water bottle cover.'

John Seton, the tallest boy in the whole school groaned and said, 'Miss, boys don't knit.'

'But men do,' Miss Wozencroft replied.

Immediately I began to consider what colours I'd choose; pale blue

and mauve in soft baby wool. If it turned out really well I'd give it as a Christmas present to my favourite aunt.

Bonnie you darling child, I'll treasure this.

'Bonnie, would you like to be knitting monitor?'

'Yes please miss.'

I jumped to my feet; I'd never been a monitor for anything before.

From a cupboard at the back of the classroom Miss Wozencroft took a brown paper bag and a cardboard box and put them on her desk.

'One pair of needles and an ounce of wool per person, please. Remember children, this is not a toy,' she held a knitting needle in front of her, 'any silly behaviour could result in a serious accident.'

The wool was like string and string coloured. My favourite aunt wouldn't call me a darling child if I gave her a hot water bottle cover made of this. It would have to be for gran

Miss Wozencroft showed us how to knit a square ten inches by ten inches in plain stitch. At the end of the afternoon the finished squares with our names pinned on them went back in the cardboard box.

'Joanna, have you handed in your square?' Miss Wozencroft asked.

'It's not finished yet miss.'

'Well finish it off at home please.'

I was knitting monitor again the following Friday. After handing out the needles and more wool I concentrated on casting-on for my new square, while daydreaming of progressing from knitting monitor to class prefect to Head Girl. At first I didn't notice the rustle of movement, heads turning, and then someone giggled. I looked up. Miss Wozencroft's neatly laced brogues stepped smartly off the dais and headed for Joanna sitting two desks back from the front.

'What is that?' She pointed to Joanna's casting-on. Her wool was bright pink.

'Mummy said there's no point me making something that won't be used, Miss Wozencroft.'

From her satchel she took out a finished bright pink square.

Miss Wozencroft's face changed colour. Two red spots appeared on her cheeks.

'Where is the piece of knitting you failed to finish last week?'

Joanna handed her the half square; all the stitches unravelling. Miss Wozencroft opened and closed her mouth twice, then holding the piece of knitting by one corner as if it were a dead mouse; she carried it back to her desk and dropped it in the waste paper basket.

She said, 'Get on with your knitting. There is merit in completing a task satisfactorily. Next week we will sew up.'

Afterwards in the playground, a crowd gathered around Joanna. Even Linda Portman joined in, banging Joanna approvingly across her shoulder blades.

'You were so brave,' someone said.

Joanna shrugged, tossing her ringlets, 'Mummy's right. It would have gone straight in the dustbin.'

Everyone agreed that theirs were going straight in the dustbin. Suddenly Joanna looked at me, standing a little apart from the group, 'Well Bonnie, what will you do with yours?'

I had a brainwave; a memory of a word gran used. My chest felt as if it would explode.

I said, 'My gran likes things that are robust.'

Joanna looked disconcerted, 'What does robust mean?'

I swallowed, a little unsure, 'Strong, hard wearing.'

She frowned, then tossed her ringlets again, 'Anyway we have electric blankets in our house.'

I made my way back into school. Under my breath I hummed 'To Be a Pilgrim', my favourite hymn. One day if I couldn't be a horse or a cowboy, I intended to be a pilgrim and do good works, but not immediately – after all Jesus didn't get going with his miracles till he was thirty.

Our classroom was empty. I hurried across to the waste paper basket and retrieved Joanna's piece of knitting. I held it against my cheek, imagining the wool feeding through Joanna's fingers.

'What are you doing?'

Joanna stood in the doorway.

'Nothing,' I said.

'That's mine – give it back.'

'No,' I said and put it in my blazer pocket.

'You *are* a flipping nutcase,' she said.

Yesterday was the last day of the Christmas term. The previous week Miss Wozencroft had brought in a post box she'd made from cardboard and red crepe paper. I wasn't sending anyone a Christmas card. I'd mentioned them to gran but she'd said, 'I'm not made of money'. I didn't expect to receive any either, but when the post was sorted out and Miss Wozencroft wearing a white beard and a Father Christmas hat had delivered them all, two cards sat on my desk. One was from John Seton who is now so tall he will probably soon be classified as a giant. This wasn't completely

unexpected – he is the least popular boy in our year and I am the least popular girl, so we make a natural pair!

The other card was from Joanna; a wintry scene of reindeers pulling sledges, snow made of silver glitter dotted the night sky and also showered my lap.

Underneath 'Happy Christmas', she'd written, 'It was the best day's play ever.' She hadn't signed her name.

I looked across to her desk by the window. Joanna was watching me. Our eyes met. She hunched up her shoulders and stuck out the tip of her tongue which made me think of the aggressive behaviour of an armadillo, although I know nothing about armadillos except that they're poor swimmers and I don't know how I know that!

I could have cried – but gran has instilled into me not to show weakness when unsure of an enemy, although at that moment Joanna Bayliss seemed like she might not be such an enemy after all.

# PARADISE

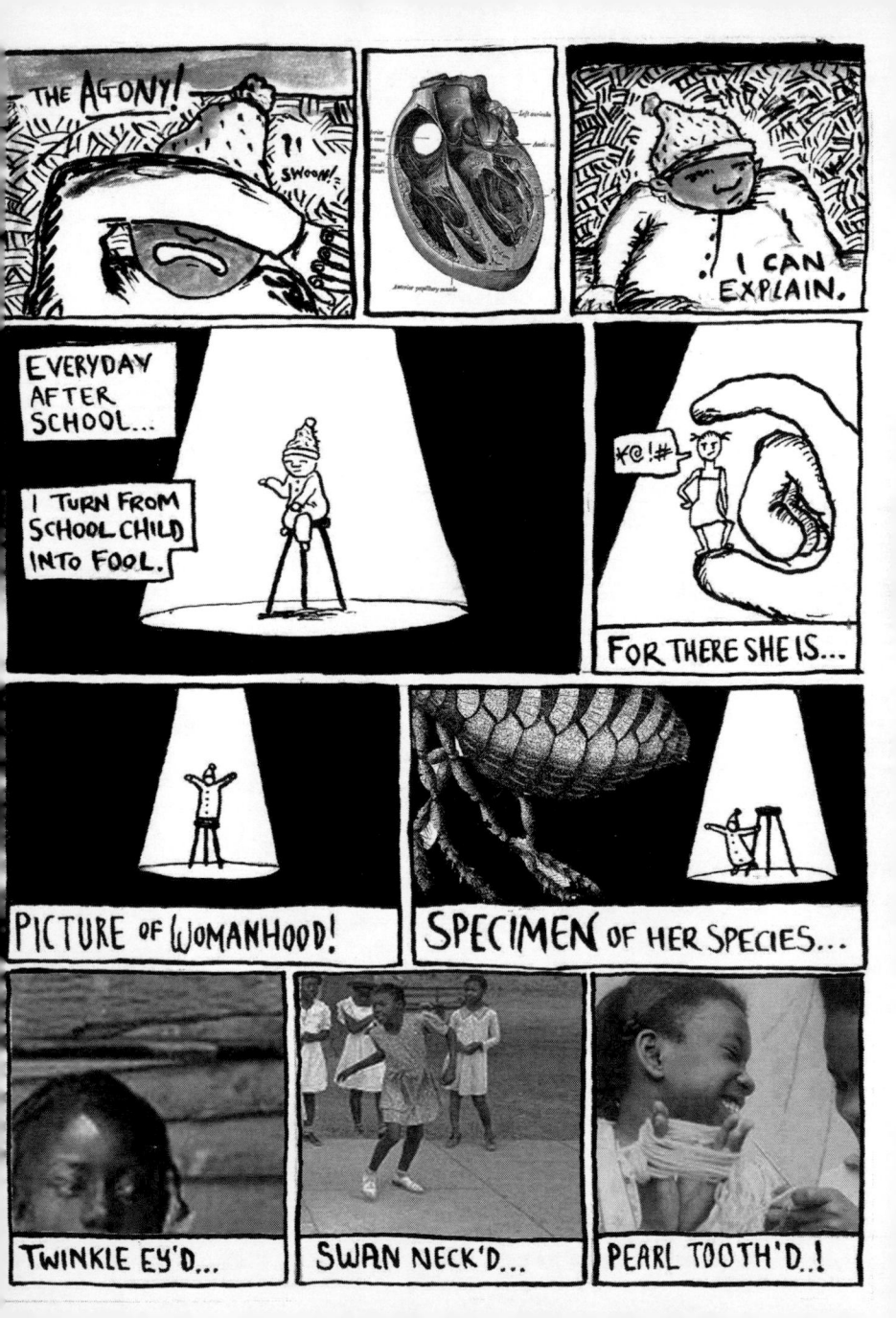

# THIS
# HOUSE
# BELIEVES

# THIS HOUSE BELIEVES

## SOPHIA BLACKWELL

I don't know anyone who's ever got through to the Lesbian and Gay Switchboard. Then again, it's not as if I've got k.d. lang, Guinevere Turner and Beth Jordache sitting in my parents' kitchen, comparing notes on the subject. I'm wondering, as always, what I'd do if they answered – whether I'd state the facts calmly, perhaps discuss the weather – the unseasonal snow that's presently caking my school skirt – or just start screaming.

When I dial this number, I'm not always so resigned. Some nights, a film with a gay character (usually ending in death, violent death, AIDS, really violent death, or even worse, eternal chronic celibacy as the wise best mate or unrequited lover of a fortysomething fag hag) has sent me upstairs, trailing the phone behind me – *Wendy! What you doing up there, love?* – crying in the silent, staccato sobs of the old-movie divas my friend Aidan worshipped.

Aidan Meeks was the only other one I knew, but we lost touch when I changed schools last year. He wasn't in my classes – I was Set One, he was pure Four, but we found each other in Drama, in the music block, on the Tube home. It wasn't just that he loved musicals and divas in big meringue dresses. It was the way he walked, the way he touched his hair, the uncertain sprawl of his mouth and the black eyes that his stepdad doled out generously. *Poor little git*, Dad said as Aidan glided down our garden path like it was a catwalk. *It's written through him like a stick of rock.*

It's written through me too, but on the inside. Even as a child, I didn't look like the tomboy I was, and was forever being told by adults that they'd expected better of me. My face is old-fashioned, a medieval illustration touched lightly with gold leaf. Ironed blonde bob, toffee eyeshadow and lip gloss, high heels and hiked-up school skirt. I pass. I pass through the corridors and changing rooms, unremarked. I am Scholarship Girl, a swishy-haired secret agent with only one secret.

Sometimes I think I'd rather be Aidan and get slammed into lockers than stand next to them trying not to look at breasts. Particularly the breasts of Sadie Thornton, who has the locker next to mine. She also has skin like hot milk dusted with nutmeg, a satin bra the old-world pink of dried roses, and a holy medal nestling between her C cups that I'd happily change places with for all eternity. Not that I've been looking.

'Wendy! You gabbing to Catherine again? I don't want to think about that bill, you two banging on about which of them dancing gaylords you fancy this week …'

Big bloke, my dad, cab-driver's paunch Mum nags him about, brown jumper under his suit jacket. He points at my skirt. 'What you been doing, making snow angels? Bit old for that, aren't you?'

I stand up, brushing at it. 'Some wankers from St. Jude's snowballed me by the church. There was loads of them, all yelling. They said school was great without me.' That last bit just slips out – I hadn't meant to tell him. It was the only part that embarrassed me. It was the only part I was scared was true.

He's half out of his jacket, but starts struggling back into it. 'Right. You reckon they're still there?'

'Dad! You can't! I'm fifteen, for God's sake.'

'You're right, sweetpea. They're just jealous. That Catholic loony bin's never gonna be great for anyone.' He takes his jacket off. 'Good day apart from that?' He always wants it to be a good day.

'Yeah. Quite funny, really, Duncan asked me to be part of this Blind Date thing the boy's school's doing for charity. Me, Nicola, and this other girl Lizzie King. They reckon she's had most of the boys' Upper Fifth already, so it'll be either me or Nicola going to Pizza Hut with some spotty freak-child. 'Confident, good-looking girls with a sense of humour,' Duncan said they wanted.'

'What they doing with you, then?'

'Laugh? I thought I'd pee my pants.'

Dad chortles, a Sid James smoker's laugh. I keep talking, trying to impress him as always. 'I'm debating against the boys tomorrow, something daft about smoking. Just cause Steve Larson-Smythe's being suspended for sparking up in front of the staff room window. That debating society's crap, we never talk about anything that matters. No nuclear disarmament, no immigration, nothing- it's always about whether we should wear these manky uniforms or not, and whether soap operas are useful social commentary or epic bollocks.'

'Well, you and Catherine like that soap with all the whinging Scousers.'

'*Brookside*, Dad. And the body under the patio stuff was classic. Even you were into that.'

'You are still friends with Catherine, aren't you?' I nod, staring out of the window. 'Good. I mean, Nicola and them are nice, but don't forget who your real friends are.'

According to Dear Anita's page in *Chic*, ten per cent of people are gay. I need that statistic on the days when Catherine doesn't return my calls

and Sadie Thornton won't look my way. I sit in class wondering who else is in that ten per cent, scared they're all in Manchester or New York or San Francisco, that the party's already swept on, leaving me here. The last lame kid in Hamelin, a forgotten Lost Boy in a short skirt.

Mum has a thing about Peter Pan. That's why I've got this ridiculous blonde name to go with my hair. There's a couple of Peter Pans in her china cabinet, pointy-chinned, twinkly and outnumbered by females in crinolines and tutus. No Amazons. No soldiers. No Lost Girls in this house but me.

The new poster on Catherine's wall — Amanda Kay, lead singer of Trash, in a scarlet boob-tube and mini-skirt, lips wet, cayenne-red hair striping her face – is a bit sexual for a straight girl, surely.

From my sleeping bag on the floor, I've been looking up at Amanda Kay and telling Catherine about Duncan Perry, the boy who asked me to be in this Blind Date fiasco. He's small and neat, with the kind of lashes they say are 'wasted on a boy,' and if you ask me, his dark flop of hair and fine-grained, feverish complexion are wasted too. I'd take them off his hands any day, but like Sadie, his skin and bones are too aristocratic for me. If I'm pretty, it's in the same way as the bus-stop girls with their buggies are, smoking their cheap, perfumey fags, ponytail fountains pulling their spines straight. The girls who don't look at me any more and mutter furiously when I walk past in my new uniform, like a swarm of pissed-off bees.

'I think he might be a bit of a bender,' I admit reluctantly. 'He's got me debating with him about this thing, Section 28. You heard of it?'

'Yeah,' she says, but something tells me not to push her on it. She's a bit prudish when it comes to sex, still sneaks her bra off under her shirt before bed. 'So this Duncan, do you fancy him?'

I'm not sure. I think he must be gay, to suggest that subject for this week's debate and to work so hard on it. As we sit in the library of Westfield Grammar, the school across the street, the boys work themselves into a libidinal frenzy at my presence and paper-planed equations are launched at our heads. I want to squeeze Duncan's smooth hand when he looks up and shakes his head at them. My partner in crime. I don't fancy him of course, but it would be nice to be liked, especially by such a pretty boy. I like the way he nods slowly when I throw him a useful statistic, how he pinches the bridge of his nose when he's tired. On the way home, I imagine myself as a lawyer in a sharp suit, making impassioned speeches, clattering anonymously through airports in stilettos. Still passing, but because I choose to this time. A luxury, a burden, a betrayal – the ability to pass can mean so many different things. I'm starting to see that.

'How come you don't fancy any boys at the moment?' I blurt out. 'It's not like there aren't any at St Jude's. And what's with the poster, anyway?'

The two of us stare at Amanda Kay like she's going to tell us.

'I just like her,' she says. 'You know I do.'

'Yeah. She's gorgeous, yeah. Do you … you know. Like girls?' I feel invulnerable somehow in the dark. The silence is thick as incense.

'Just one,' she says. For a weird minute, I wonder if it's me. 'Amanda, that is. I know it's just a phase. I'm not worrying about it.'

It's OK to have a crush on a poster-girl. Even Judy Blume says so. It is not OK to sit in class imagining what you'd do to Sadie Thornton if the Bomb was about to drop. When she gives me chewing gum on the bus it is not normal to take it out of my mouth later, mould it into a tiny jade heart and keep it in a box under my bed with cut-out letters from magazines beginning, 'Dear Anita, I like boys but I think I am …'

'Wendy? I used to wonder if you were gay. But you're not, are you? If you like this Duncan?'

'He's all right.' I know she wants to hear more. 'But I … if I tell you something, do you promise never to tell anybody? Even if we had a massive fight?'

The room's soft darkness seeps into my blood. I'm safe here, in a way I'm not at school under the carved roll-calls, or at home with the china ballerinas and Dad booming from room to room, or in the streets with snowballs flying at my skull.

I don't know why I'm telling her. Perhaps I feel I owe her something for leaving her behind. I don't go into details about the Switchboard, my end-of-the-world sexual fantasies starring Sadie or the times I sneak into the bargain bookstore and dare myself to shoplift *The Art of Lesbian Love* because I'm not exactly sure how to do it. But I tell her enough.

'Did you know?' I finish.

I know she'll say yes. She does.

'You don't think we've fucked up our friendship forever, do you?' I ask.

'No,' she says. 'Course not. No. Did you see *Brookside*?'

'Say hello to Number Three!' bellows our MC, a cocky little sod called Edward Reece who looks like the Artful Dodger, rattles with Ritalin and was presumably chosen because he's one of the three Westfield boys who can talk to girls without being sick – Duncan Perry and Steve Larson-Smythe, the Staff-Room Window Smoker, being the other two.

Steve is our suitor today, the one I have the honour of a pizza with if I win. Duncan is at the front, staring up at me while I try to brace my thighs against the seat of my stool so they simultaneously look narrow, keep me

upright and conceal my gusset. I may have to forget one of these options but I can't decide which.

Half the crowd have been chanting, 'Three! Three! Three!' since I tottered onto the stage. The others are shouting for Number One – Nicola, my sort-of-friend. Brunette, horsey teeth, handy with a tennis racket.

No one is shouting for Lizzie King, who has her skirt rolled and folded in half at her waist, clinching her wishbone thighs, and is chewing gum like a serial killer.

I can't concentrate. It's too much. It's too much because when I arrived, Duncan came up and told me he was sorry, the Section 28 debate was cancelled.

'Just too controversial,' he said in that light, posh voice. 'Besides, one of our teachers is totally bent and he wasn't keen on it at all. Thought it would bring him attention, so I had to … anyway, sorry, Wendy. They'll get rid of it anyway, you know that. It's all over bar the shouting.'

It's too much because yesterday, on the way home, two St. Jude's kids started yelling at me again. With a practised posh-girl flip of my hair, hoisting my book-bag higher, I strode on, but then I heard that word again and again, that nasal insect buzz. *Lezzer.*

Catherine had told them. No snowballs this time, just insults. I tried to hold my face together, not to break into a run. In the kitchen, I dialled the Switchboard's number. I knew Catherine's number by heart too, but I didn't call it.

In the still kitchen with the dial tone humming, I heard myself speak. 'This house believes that Section 28 should be abolished.' By the time Mum and Dad got home, my tears had dried and I was word-perfect, but I'd barely had time to think about Blind Date- which, of course, had

not been cancelled. No one gets offended by girls being auctioned off. Harmless fun.

'Number One,' says Steve, clearly itching for a fag. 'My favourite subject is Maths because I like putting two and two together. If you gave me extra tuition ...' groans from the crowd, '... what subject would you choose, and why?'

'Well,' chirps Nicola wholesomely, 'everyone knows I love Games!'

Roars from the crowd. She makes a little moue at them. 'So why don't you put away those books and work up a sweat with me on the field?' Unbridled baying from the Westfield boys. You wouldn't think she had it in her. Maybe we'll be proper friends some day.

'Number Two?'

'French,' growls Lizzie. 'My grammar's not great, but I know about kissing, and I like getting my tongue round unfamiliar things.'

The roar becomes an avalanche. The teacher at the back looks like he's about to intervene, but then thinks better of it. I bet he's the gay one.

'Number Three?'

'Well,' I burble, 'Lady Barbara's girls are all domestic goddesses, so I'd give you a crash course in cookery and a little light housekeeping. I'll heat up your crumpets, you can chintz up my bedroom – and you know how housework is, just a couple of months later we'll have to do it again.'

The crowd cracks up. I plant myself more securely on the stool, look down into the audience, and see two things that shake me- one, that Sadie is looking fixedly at me. The kind of look I got from the old ladies of my childhood who'd Expected Better. And two, that little Duncan, perfectly groomed in his rich spotted silk tie, is not looking at me. I can't see Steve Larson-Smythe, but Duncan can, and he's making the most of it. Interesting.

We keep on batting away pointless questions with cheery innuendo like blazered Club 18-30 reps. What objects do we always carry? How do we relax? If we were a film, what would we be? (Nicola's *Four Weddings*, I'm *True Romance*. Lizzie is *Basic Instinct*).

Final question. 'As you may know,' Steve says portentously, 'I'm a bit of a freedom fighter.'

'You're a wanker,' says a boy whose recently broken voice makes him sound like a stoned opera singer.

'Give us a fag, Steve,' another one yells. Clearly they take his debates as seriously as I do.

'What cause would you fight for, and why? That's to Number Two.'

'Binge drinking,' says Lizzie. 'I think it should be mandatory.'

'Number One?'

'The RSPCA. I love animals. And if you choose me as your Blind Date, you'll find that I'm a bit of an animal too.' Cheers and whoops.

My heart pounds. What do I believe in? 'Well, Steve,' I hear myself say, 'I reckon I'd abolish Section 28. I mean, as long as it's around, we're going to have politicians talking about how upstanding young men like you are going to be 'sucked into a gay lifestyle,' with no hint of irony. Also, why would we want to imitate our teachers- like, are you wearing tweed and leather patches? You know what else I'd fight for? Gays in the military. Your school would be a lot less crowded.'

Silence, then a rustle of scared laughter. I swing down, probably flashing the front row.

'We're not finished yet,' Edward Kay stage-whispers.

'I am.'

'Just ... oh bugger it ... right, Ladies and Gentlemen!' Edward brings the lucky bachelor forward. Duncan shouts, 'Three!' The girls join in, even

Sadie Thornton. They won't agree with me, but they acknowledge I'm good enough to date. It's something. It may be all I'm getting.

Unsurprisingly, Steve chooses Nicola. Lizzie sashays past Steve and gooses him. When it's my turn, I put my arms round him gracefully, smiling like it's Oscar night.

I don't think any gay teacher cancelled the debate. Seeing Duncan's face as he looked up at Steve, enjoying a moment's anonymity, the excuse to look and love without accusations- it reminded me of me. He bottled out. *Poor little git. It's written through him like a stick of rock.*

As my higher-than-regulation heels carry me back into the crowd, I know Duncan Perry is going to ask me out. And I know I'm going to say no, but perhaps he'd like to come over and watch old movies some time.

'Wendy! ... Catherine's on the phone.' I just stand there, all my bravado gone in the time it took to open the door. 'Go on, girl,' he says impatiently. I shake my head. 'What? You two had a row or ... she'll call you back, Cath.' He puts the phone down. 'What is it, sweetpea? Those little scrotes from your old school upset you again? Go on, you tell me.'

Here he is, the man who washed my back in the bath, taught me to drive on North London's industrial estates, and held me in the pool while I wriggled and clung. He holds me like that now, but I feel like a mannequin, painted and steely, so heavy I might knock him over.

'What is it?' he asks again. 'Spit it out. It can't be that bad. Not compared to what I got up to at your age.' He pauses. 'You're not ... you're not in trouble, are you?'

'No. God, no. Um, do you reckon ... do you think we could go and sit down? Could you get Mum?'

I can't quite believe I'm doing this. But still, it'll be all over soon. Bar the shouting.

Dad calls up the stairs and I fill the kettle, marvelling at the steadiness of my hands. I have five minutes of my old life left. I clear my throat, prepare myself, breathe. This House Believes.

It's five in the morning, the light thick and backlit blue. Never-Never Land.

It's not my frilly girl's name that made me hate Peter Pan. Not even my mother's tacky ornaments. It's the end of the story. Peter, ageless, heartless ready to party, comes to Wendy's daughter's window- and, of course, she goes with him.

I'm going too, one of these days. I'm going to find the other lost ones. I'm going to be in a bar one day and look over at a soft-mouthed boy, glitter on his cheekbones like an angel's finger traced them, and say, *Aidan? Aidan Meeks? Is that you?*

Dad looked ten years older and kept saying it didn't matter. Mum shook her head. 'It's so hard,' she said. 'These people, they're messed-up, mental. I don't want you with one of them.'

I sat watching my tea grow cold, wondering when I'd last cried in front of them, and why I couldn't stop.

'Everything's hard,' Dad said. 'Life is hard. We gave you the best start we could ...'

I watched them digesting the fact that education wasn't going to save me. I was surprised too. It was my only contingency plan.

'Wendy,' Dad said, 'it might be ... say you went to a couple of parties, met some boys ...'

'No,' I said, and 'No,' Mum said at the same time. She shook her head.

'She's always been like this.'

When she went up the stairs, Dad and I sat together.

'Wendy,' he said, 'you can hold your head up while you drink your fucking tea.'

Mum took me to the pantomime of Peter Pan when I was six. When her daughter's gone, Wendy – all grown up, a sensible mother now – walks into the empty room. I remember the stage bathed in indigo, the woman stopping when she sees the white curtain belling back from the window.

As a kid, I'd thought that was a mean thing to do to an old friend – but perhaps she'd known for years that this was how it would be. Maybe, before she went and shut the window, she looked up into the sky, to see if she could catch a glimpse of vanishing light. But that little girl's room would still be empty.

# EXPENDABLE CHARACTERS

# EXPENDABLE CHARACTERS

## HELEN SANDLER

The sword suited her. So did the doublet. In fact, Rachel looked even more dashing in costume than she did in uniform, which was saying something. Alex was revelling in their time alone in the school hall, rehearsing their double-act away from the interfering teacher who was directing the show. Much of their wordplay might be meaningless to a modern audience, but Alex liked to think that the sheer wit and charisma emanating from herself and Rachel would impel the crowd to cackle at their codpiece puns.

They both had strong voices and their lines were bouncing off the walls. Rachel made a knightly flourish with her expressive right hand as she performed her next line; Alex held her teasing gaze and stepped closer to fire back her favourite riposte, imagining all the while that they were centre stage at the Royal Exchange.

At the end of the scene, her new friend grinned broadly at her. 'We are the best expendable characters,' she declared, 'ever to appear on the Shakespearean stage … in a secondary school context.'

Alex glowed and preened. She might be going to her friend Laura's house after school and out with Paul at the weekend, but it would be Rachel's words that found their way into her diary when she next wrote it up.

\*\*\*

'Do you think your Alex Didsbury has started something with that Rachel girl from the Lower Fifth?' Miss Salmon asked Miss Finch, refilling her wine glass.

'Oh you and your baby dykes,' said Miss Finch in mock irritation. 'You're more interested in their adolescent fumblings than in ours.'

'So you think there are adolescent fumblings going on?'

'Frankly, Irene, I don't think they'd know the word "sapphic" if you chalked it on the blackboard during double Greek.'

'Well, I saw them in the hall at lunchtime, rehearsing in full male drag, just the two of them.'

'That's because I told them to do exactly that,' said Miss Finch, pouring salt from a designated eggcup onto the middle of her plate. She liked salt as much as Miss Salmon liked spice. 'They have some rather tedious scenes together and I don't see why the other girls should have to sit in the wings while they show off their elocution every other day. They can manage perfectly well without me.'

'They're not the only ones,' muttered Miss Salmon.

'This basket looks dirty!' said Laura, the least sophisticated and most sex-obsessed of the friends. They were in the queue at the Co-op in their own clothes, having changed out of their uniforms together in the cloakroom.

Alex wasn't entirely sure what Laura meant and didn't particularly want to know, but Katy chipped in with, 'Yeah, we're all going to go back to yours, drink the wine and then take turns with the cucumber!'

If they carried on with such immature jokes, thought Alex, the cashier might notice they were underage. Then again, the content was not

dissimilar to her stage dialogue with Rachel. Every time she thought of Rachel she had a funny feeling in her stomach … probably nerves about the performance. She tried to join in with the others as they all walked round to Laura's, where they would have the house to themselves for the evening. She would find it easier when she'd had a drink and started to relax.

As it happened she relaxed a bit too much. She was feeling quite hazy as she lay back on Laura's bed and watched the tassled lampshade sway from side to side. Laura and Katy were arguing about something to do with Culture Club. Something about the lyrics to the latest single.

'Alex!' Laura shouted at the top of her voice, trying to get her attention.

'What?' Alex rolled on her side and stuck her head over the edge of the bed for a good look at Laura, whose face was looming in and out of focus.

'Ohhh!' With a shriek, Laura veered away.

'Oh my god, were you going to kiss her?' squealed Katy.

'What?'

'Yeah,' said Laura, 'it was like you were going to kiss me!' She laughed drunkenly. 'You're weird.' She got up and stared at Alex. 'Weeiiird. I only wanted to know the words to "Church of the Poison Mind".'

By Monday it was all forgotten and Alex had another rehearsal to look forward to. She and Rachel had agreed to run their lines over and over at lunchtime, until they were confident that they could deliver them at speed without tripping up. There was only a week to go till the first night and Alex had a tendency to get nervy around that time. She was already having dreams in which she didn't know her lines or was pushed onstage in the wrong play.

Rachel seemed to have no such fears. She had appeared in a professional production the previous term and was expecting to go to drama school eventually. Her confidence brought out Alex's expansive side, made her bigger onstage and funnier off it.

'I don't think that was right,' Alex said now. 'The line before last – I think I lost a word. Let me just look at my script.' As she walked back to the desk where she had left her things, Rachel intercepted her, waving her own script with that exaggerated flourish she used onstage.

'Sirrah, allow me!'

'Away, thou clotpole!' Alex parried her away but Rachel hit back. They pushed and wrestled, the classroom furniture shunting away from them, till their arms locked over their heads. Time stood still. They were panting into each other's faces.

'What is going on here?' The piercing voice of Miss Finch broke them apart.

'Nothing, Miss Finch, we're just practising our swordplay,' said Rachel, composed in an instant.

'That's not what it looked like,' said the teacher, her face a picture of outrage.

'We'll put everything back where it was,' Rachel added with an angelic smile.

'Yes, you certainly will. And you will not "rehearse" on your own any more,' said Miss Finch.

'Why not?' asked Alex.

'Yes, why not?' asked Rachel.

'You know why not. If you cannot maintain propriety then you cannot be trusted to be alone together.'

'Are you getting at something?'

There was a silence.

Rachel was not to be left unanswered. 'Miss Finch? Are you accusing us of something?'

'Go outside now, girls,' said the teacher, her face shutting down.

As she and Rachel passed Miss Finch in the doorway, Alex saw three girls from her year standing in the corridor, all ears.

'What exactly went on today?' Miss Salmon asked when Miss Finch came in the door at 6.30.

'I stayed late for rehearsal, as usual on a Monday.'

'I mean,' she said pointedly, 'what happened at lunchtime?'

'What?' Miss Finch put down her briefcase and poured herself a gin and tonic.

'It's all round the school that you laid into those girls. People seem to think you said something … odd.'

'They were fighting in the classroom.'

'Fighting?'

'Playing at fighting, I should say.'

'Oh, was it steamy?'

'Irene! You're as bad as they are.'

'So, what *did* you say to them?'

'I told them they couldn't be left alone together.'

'Well, you can see how that could be misinterpreted.'

'Yes, thank you, dear. I'll do the English sentence deconstruction. You can stick to the Greek.'

'I do believe you're frightened of the idea that something might be going on between them,' said Miss Salmon triumphantly.

'And you're not? You'd like the whole school to be on some lesbian rampage, would you?'

'It doesn't reflect on you, you know.'

'Either there's nothing going on or there's scandal in the school and everyone is under suspicion. There is no middle way.'

'You sound like a paranoid nutcase.'

'Thank you for your cutting analysis. When you force your own way out of the closet, you may lecture me.'

Alex and Rachel were celebrities by the time the bell rang for the end of school – for having stood up to Miss Finch or for having been up to something 'weird', depending who was telling the story. It all made the official rehearsal with the teacher somewhat awkward and Alex was relieved to get out to the pub afterwards with Paul. Snogging him in the bus shelter killed time until the 48 arrived and it gave her a thrill in the cold air but there was no way she would have taken up his invitation to go back to his house at that hour. She waved to him from the top of the nightbus and glided through the city in a cider daze, then jumped off a stop early for a portion of chips and gravy.

The food was wrapped in a newspaper story about a homosexual politician who had got into trouble. As she shovelled the slimy chips to her mouth at the kitchen table, Alex read the piece three times, wondering if many people were homosexual.

She wiped her hands on the paper, threw it in the bin, turned off the kitchen light and stumbled up to bed, avoiding the squeaky stair so as not to wake her parents. She would be in trouble in the morning for coming home late but she might be able to knock half an hour off her actual arrival time under questioning.

Lying in the dark under her brown flowered duvet, Alex tried to comprehend the bizarre happenings of the last few days. Girls' faces, accusations, laughter... But none of it making any sense. She thought of how she and Rachel had ranted their way through their scenes at lunchtime, how they had launched themselves at each other... There was something... something she wanted to happen.

But didn't life always get strange and intense, just before a performance? Probably everything would seem better when they got the first night out of the way.

# AMBER

# AMBER

## THE ALBERT KENNEDY TRUST

I was born in Chorley. I'm a late '80s girl. I'm forever young. My earliest memory is from when I was about three or four years old. Me and my Grandma used to catch the bus to town every Saturday morning. My Grandma had trouble walking upstairs but she always walked up to the top deck with me. We sat on the top of the double decker bus and she gave me fudge. It makes my heart melt every time I remember that. I know she cared for me.

My childhood was very different from what I see as a childhood. I can't really remember much about the early years. I do remember secondary school. I went to the local school. I attended every day like a good girl should. But as the years went on, when I grew older, I felt ill. Not like having a cold ill. A different kind of ill. It turned out to be a mental illness. I am ninety-seven percent better now, by the way! But growing up I didn't know this, so as I got older things at school became difficult and I didn't know why.

I didn't really like school. I found life back then really difficult. I don't really visit that place anymore as I'm over it. One subject I really enjoyed was Child Development. It was about learning how the baby or child developed physically and at what stages. Although most of it was paper-based studying in school I really enjoyed it.

I have heard a little bit about anti-gay bullying in places like America and Canada, but not in the UK. I have not experienced anything like that, thank goodness. I have never witnessed anything with regards to someone being gay in school. I was bullied at school, but nobody ever knew about me being gay. I didn't know myself. When I was at school I never saw anything about support groups for LGBT people. And if they had and people saw them looking at them they would more than likely get beaten up for looking at the poster. I do think society is more accepting of lesbian women than gay men.

I suppose I always knew about my sexuality but I was never really sure. It's difficult being young with everything going on in life. My mother knows. The older generation, they will never know. I know what the older generations of my family are like towards LGBT people.

I have been with The Albert Kennedy Trust since I was eighteen years old. I am an Albert Kennedy girl! I started off meeting a mentor once a week for two years. We did so much good work. He was a good friend, someone to talk to who wouldn't judge me. We were very similar. We got on so well. As I say about him – 'he's like me in a man'. He is a legend! Now I do talks for AKT, and I see a student social worker once a week. I thank AKT for being there.

It's pretty good going over personal things like this. It is stressful sometimes, but I am coping. I am happy. I want to continue studying and hopefully get a job helping people. I've always found learning and taking things in and storing them to be difficult. It still is, to this day. But I'm still learning. It's an ongoing process. I am getting there. And when I do I will be so clever the world won't know what's hit it!

# INDEX OF CONTRIBUTORS

## HELEN SANDLER

Helen Sandler has written two novels, *The Touch Typist* and *Big Deal*, and edited Lambda-winning anthologies. Her poems and stories have appeared in *Brand, Chroma* and *Smoke*. She is an MC at London's Bar Wotever and runs Tollington Press, publishing new writing by women.

tollingtonpress.co.uk

## JAY BERNARD

Jay Bernard is a writer and cartoonist who divides her time between Oxford and London. She is currently co-editor of *Dissocia Zine* and a student of English Literature. She has been featured in two anthologies, *Voice Recognition* and *City State*. Her first collection of poetry *Your Sign is Cuckoo, Girl* was PBS pamphlet choice for summer 2008. Jay is also a recipient of the Foyle's Young Poet of the Year Award and was champion at the London Respect Slam. Her first exhibition is scheduled to take place in St Andrews, in March 2011.

brrnrrd.wordpress.com

## KAREN MCLEOD

Karen McLeod is the author of the award winning *In Search of the Missing Eyelash* published by Vintage. She is a cabaret performer and recently retired air stewardess. She has worked as a cleaner, a life model and a balloon seller. She lives in south London with her record player..

karenmcleod.info

## SOPHIA BLACKWELL

Sophia Blackwell is a performance poet who has appeared at Glastonbury, The Big Chill, WOMAD and Wychwood Festivals and venues such as The Roundhouse and Soho Revue Bar. Her debut collection, *Into Temptation*, is available from Tollington Press and her journalism has been published in *Trespass*, *Pen Pusher*, and *Rising*.

## STELLA DUFFY

Stella Duffy has written twelve novels, forty short stories, and eight plays. Her latest novel, *Theodora*, is published by Virago in summer 2010. In addition to her writing work, Stella is an actor and theatre director. She lives in south London with her wife, the writer Shelley Silas.

stelladuffy.wordpress.com

## VG LEE

VG Lee has written three novels including *Diary of a Provincial Lesbian*, and a short story collection *As You Step Outside* published by Tollington Press. She is also a stand-up comedian and a finalist in the Hackney Empire New Act of the Year 2010 competition.

# BOYS & GIRLS

# HOW TO ORDER

Please email sales@glasshousebooks.co.uk or call 020 7001 1177. Alternatively, you can buy online at glasshousebooks.co.uk.

For trade enquiries please contact Turnaround on 020 8829 3000 or email orders@turnaround-uk.com

100
£10
9781907536007

BLOODY VAMPIRES
£10
9781907536663

33
£15
IN 2 VOLUMES

BOYS & GIRLS
£10
9781907536090

# A GLASSHOUSE BOOKS COLLABORATION

Design by Eren Butler
Edited by Paul Burston
Managed by Bobby Nayyar
Published in association with The Albert Kennedy Trust
Typeset in Arno Pro and Champagne & Limousines
First published 14. 07. 2010.
'Jail Bait' by Stella Duffy was first published in *Britpulp*, Sceptre, 1999
Joe Storey-Scott photograph by Maciej Falski
Paul Burston photograph by Adrian Lourie

ISBN 978-1-907536-09-0

Glasshouse Books
58 Glasshouse Fields
Flat 30, London
E1W 3AB

glasshousebooks.co.uk
facebook.com/GlasshouseBooks

In some circumstances we may be able to provide limited support to young people facing homelessness through our *Emergency Support Pack*, and for those young people we have worked with for some time we can, in certain circumstances, provide access to our *Rainbow Starter Pack* to help with the costs of moving into independent living.

We also offer training and audit to mainstream housing and homelessness organizations to ensure they treat LGBT people with respect and fairness, as part of our '*Making a Difference*' quality mark scheme.

We have recently developed a new project with funding from the *Forced Marriages Unit* in response to an increasing number of young people from faith backgrounds contacting AKT who are being threatened with honour killings by their families who cannot accept their sexual orientation.

TO SUPPORT OUR WORK BY MAKING OR DONATION OR THROUGH VOLUNTEERING YOUR TIME PLEASE VISIT US ONLINE WWW.AKT.ORG.UK OR CALL 020 7831 6562

LONDON OFFICE

Unit 203 Hatton Square Business Centre
16/16a Baldwins Gardens
London, EC1N 7RJ
Tel. 020 7831 6562
Email: contact@akt.org.uk

MANCHESTER OFFICE

4th Floor, Princess House
105 107 Princess Street
Manchester, M1 6DD
Tel: 0161 228 3308
Email: contact@akt.org.uk

PLEASE CONSIDER MAKING A DONATION TO AKT FOR EVERY £20 DONATED, WE CAN PROVIDE A YOUNG PERSON WTH A SAFE PLACE TO SLEEP FOR A NIGHT.

THANK YOU!

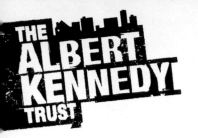

REGISTERED CHARITY NO. 1093815

SINCE 1989 AKT HAS SUPPORTED LESBIAN, GAY, BISEXUAL AND TRANS (LGBT) YOUNG PEOPLE (UP TO 25 YEARS OLD) WHO ARE HOMELESS OR LIVING IN A HOSTILE ENVIRONMENT. MANY OF OUR YOUNG PEOPLE HAVE BEEN REJECTED BY THEIR PARENTS OR BULLIED AT SCHOOL JUST FOR BEING BRAVE ENOUGH TO COME OUT AS GAY.

WE PROVIDE:  Safe and supportive homes with LGBT Carers through our *Supported Lodgings Scheme*. We also have a range of organizations we refer to in cases where we cannot supply accommodation.

More informal support by helping young people build positive independent futures through *mentoring and befriending*.

*Advocacy, information and support* by phone, face to face or email: to help young people achieve their own tenancy, employment or return to education.

Opportunities for young people to develop life skills to help them secure employment, their own tenancy or a place in higher education through our *accredited training programme*.

FOR MORE INFORMATION, PLEASE LOG ONTO OUR WEBSITE AT

# WWW.AKT.ORG.UK